I0459950

Tempest© Copyright 2019 Renee Joiner

ISBN: 978-1-948834-94-0

Cover design by Michele Barrow-Belisle

Published by Oshun Publications

www.oshunpublications.com

TEMPEST

RENEE JOINER

Oshun
Publications

Contents

Join My Newsletter

Get Updates, Freebies & Giveaways

RENEEJOINERAUTHOR.COM/NEWSLETTER

ONE

Tell Me What You Know

A DEATHLY CALM SETTLED INTO MELONI'S BONES. IT wasn't the sort of stillness that came with killing. No, that was different. This calmness came with invisibility. She became one with the air, with the roaring winds and the sand that stretched as far as the eye could see. She became one with the structures she had to climb. The jumps she had to make. Never a noise, never a rustle in the sand. She was a ghost, and no human ever saw her unless she wanted to be seen.

Meloni tucked her feet under her. She's been sitting on the old, abandoned elevator since sunrise. The heat was starting to get unbearable. The elevator shaft must have once belonged to a large hotel of sorts. It was hard to tell which buildings were which nowadays. Humans might have grown resistant to the effects the elements had over the years. Still, the buildings didn't have that ability. The shell of the shaft had either been stripped or corroded away, and all that was left was an iron skeleton. A thin sheet of corrugated iron on the very top of the shaft shielded her from the scorching midday sun, but it did little to keep the heated wind away from her. It was time for her to get a move on if she wanted to make it home by night-fall. The sun was her biggest enemy during the daytime, but at night was when the creatures came out to play.

Spending the morning hours memorizing the length of shifts and routes the guards took, Meloni knew she had a good idea of what to expect. She looked down at the mercenary encampment below. If they haven't seen her by now, she was sure her presence would go unnoticed until she decided otherwise.

It wasn't a very big encampment. There were ten guards at key points of the fence surrounding it. Corru-gated iron shielding them from gunfire, but that also meant that there were blind spots. Spots she could easily use to her advantage. The guards didn't move much, and that was a colossal mistake on their part. It made them predictable. Meloni knew exactly where which guard was at what time. It was too easy.

In the main building, half the hotel Meloni assumed belonged to the elevator shaft was draped with curtains of different bleached-out colors. She wondered briefly where the other half of the building went but shook the idea from her head quickly. Trying to make sense of such things wasn't going to help her now. There wasn't a lot left in the world that made any sense anyway. It just existed, or it didn't. There was no reason for either.

The sheets on the building did little to hide whatever was inside as they were a good foot or two from each floor. She assumed it was to keep the sun out and not prying eyes. There were seven stories, the eighth only having half a wall. Each story held a different commander and bunks. The bottom one was the kitchen. None of the people inside revealed themselves, which either meant they were busy inside, or sensitive to the sun. Meloni has seen people sporting blisters the size of eggs on their faces. Some people, like the building, just didn't grow immune to the elements. This meant that she had to be as far away as she could before sunset. The Nighters were far more feral than the immune.

Meloni checked her weapons. Four knives, a gun, and seven bullets. It was enough to defend herself when things got ugly. She only hoped that she'd get in and out before that happened. There was a building about half a mile East. She had the mind to check it out before climbing the shaft to spy on the encampment. It was an old recording studio. Upon further investigation, she noticed that the soundproofing was still intact. If she could just get a guard there without being noticed, she could interrogate him without worrying about him alerting his friends.

She watched the guard at the base of the shaft. He was scrawny-looking, probably malnutrition. They didn't look like the sort who knew where to hunt or harvest proper food. This encampment was one of the many that housed the most dimwitted mercenaries. Meloni could use that to her advantage. This guard was the only one stationed outside the gate. It was useful for her. It meant that she didn't have to smuggle him out the gate. This was going to be too easy. Lead the guard to the studio; grill him for information, then circle back to gather some supplies from the kitchen if there was enough time left. Meloni had to move fast.

With the grace of a gymnast, she used the corroded iron from the shaft to lower herself level by level. The placing of her hands had to be precise. God only knew what illnesses she would get if the iron cut her. Never mind the attention her fall would attract. Every possible outcome played out in her head. With every level, the result became more gruesome until she was on the level above the guard, and the image in her head showed her running through the desert, a hoard of Immunes behind her, and the Nighters following as soon as the sun hid behind the dunes. What happened to her, what happened to her body, was not a pretty sight.

Shaking the thoughts from her head, she pulled her mask over her face, the hand-painted skull resembling something from nightmares. With her face covered, she was nothing but a black wraith with a white skull where her face once was. Meloni moved like ink in water, the hood over her head not moving an inch as she dropped down behind the guard and pressed a knife to his throat.

"One word and your blood will seep into the sand, got it?" Her voice was raspy, partially because she wanted to mask it as much as possible, and partly because she hadn't spoken out loud in days. The mercenary must have been smarter than she thought as he threw his hands in the air and swallowed. She felt the slight movement below her blade. It caused a thin trickle of blood to escape his split skin.

Meloni had timed the attack just right. It was a few minutes before the guards change shifts, and the guards were casual enough not to worry about one taking off a few minutes early. If the other guard got to the post, she and her mercenary friends would have been long gone.

She kept them to the shadows of the building, to the blind spots where she knew the guards couldn't see them. One well-aimed bullet was all it took, and then all of her hard work would be for naught. She came this far. There was no going back. She couldn't get killed just yet. There was still too much to do, still too many mysteries to solve.

Her mind was busy enough to pass the time. They were at the studio sooner than she had realized. Meloni pushed the guard inside and barricaded the door behind them. No one was going to interrupt them. If he knew something, he was going to talk one way or another. Nothing was going to get in the way of that. Nothing.

"Take your top off and get on the chair," she commanded. When she registered his stunned expression, she rolled her eyes. "You won't be that lucky. Just do it or I will do it for you."

As silent as a mute, the mercenary took his vest, followed by his shirt off. Along the way, he had lost his rifle. She didn't know when perhaps he was leaving a trail for his friends. She should have paid better attention to him instead of fantasizing about her own death. That mistake might just be what caused it. She huffed as she pulled two coils of rope from her backpack. His eyes grew wide. "Sit your ass down, asshole, or you won't like the consequences."

"Y-you're the Ghost," he stammered. She hated that word. She hated that they called her the Ghost. A ghost meant that she was dead, that she was merely the soul of someone who had already left the world. She preferred something like wraith or shadow. Something that didn't come to be by the death of something else. Something that just existed.

"If you know who I am, you know what's going to happen if you don't do exactly as I say," she said as she played along, expertly tying knots in the rope.

"You don't have to tie me up," the man said. "I'll tell you everything."

Meloni laughed. "This isn't for now, sweetie. It's for later." She pointed toward the chair in the middle of the room that she had placed there on her initial inspection of the place. He finally sat down quietly.

Having time to take in her surroundings, she inspected the red, padded walls. They were stylishly finished, and empty hooks held the ghost of guitars. Raiders must have taken everything valuable from this place long ago. "This was where people recorded music once, you know?" she said, more to herself than to her captive. "Artists used to come here and record their albums. Do you even know what I'm talking about?" The man shook his head, and she sighed. "Of course, you don't. You lot are as uncultured as camels. Now..." She stepped toward him, a grin plastered on her face. She knew that he couldn't see it, but his body went rigid anyway as if sensing the maliciousness of her smile.

"What do you want from me?" The man said as she stepped closer to him. She could see his blue eyes, wide with fear. The room was dimly lit by a window on the far end, but she could still see the color of his eyes. So blue that it looked animated. All the pigment was drained from it thanks to years of being exposed in this wasteland and bad breeding. He was skinny for a guard, even skinnier than her, and had tattoos that covered every inch of him. A sandworm snaked its way down from his abdomen and into his pants. She shuddered to think where that tattoo led.

"Your kind took someone from me," Meloni spat, leaning down, so her mask was mere inches from his face. "I want him back."

"I don't know what you're talking about," he lied. She knew he was lying. He had to be because if he wasn't...

"I am the immediate threat. Tell me or the head of the sandworm will be chopped off." She pointed her knife to his crotch in emphasis.

The man swallowed. "I might have heard something about a man being taken by the Scorpion."

Meloni's blood chilled. This was bad; this was very, very bad. If the Scorpion was involved, there was no way of surviving the encounter. But why would the Scorpion bother? There was nothing they had that he wanted. They stayed out of his way; they didn't mingle in his affairs. Everybody knew not to piss the Scorpion off. Everyone knew that... It made no sense. "Bullshit," she spat. "He had no business with the Scorpion."

"If it breathes, it has business with the Scorpion," the man grinned. Meloni punched him before having the time to stop herself. She wasn't sure if she was punching him because she needed more information, or because she was frustrated thinking that the Scorpion might be involved.

"Tell me what you know," she hissed.

"There is one person we fear more than you, Ghost, and that is the Scorpion. I'd rather die by your hands than face his wrath." The man had a point. She would have done the same in his situation. "Besides, I have nothing to tell. I only heard about a man with blond hair being taken South."

"Blond," she repeated his words. Blond, not raven-haired. Not like the person she was after. It wasn't the same person. She let out a guttural laugh, one that caused every hair on a person's body to stand upright. "I'm not looking for a blond," she said simply. "The man I'm after has black hair. The color of raven feathers."

"Did I say blond? I meant black hair," the man quickly corrected. His nervous twitch made her palm itch. He didn't know anything. He was feeding her information to keep her happy.

She has had enough. "You don't know shit, do you?" she sighed and pulled the rope taught in her hands. "I guess there's only one thing left to do with you."

TWO

Water and a Medic

ALARMS SOUNDED IN THE DISTANCE, BUT MELONI WAS already too far away for anyone to track her. For once, she was grateful that the sand left no footprints.

She wanted to kill the mercenary. God knew it would have been one less evil to deal with, but with all the blood on her hands already, she didn't have the heart to add to it. Not unless it was absolutely necessary. Besides, leaving him alive to give his men a message was better than leaving them a dead body and earning a bounty on her head in return.

Meloni tied him to the front door of the studio and told him to wait ten minutes before he alerted his men. She noticed he had a radio which he was too stupid or star struck to use when she took him. It was an error on her part. Her mind was all over the place, and it was starting to show. Mistakes were beginning to ooze from the cracks in her demeanor. Ten minutes. She knew he'd obey. She could tell he valued his life more than his honor, and right then, she was the biggest threat. Ten minutes gave her enough time to cover the ground between the studio and a safe hiding spot. She picked up his rifle he had dropped along the way and found with no little satisfaction, that the magazine was full. Small mercies, she thought.

Having a shortage of paper and ink, Meloni had to make do with what she had; a knife and a bare-chested individual. As much as she wanted to carve the message into his chest, she knew the blood would make it far too hard to read. So, she cut open his hand and used his own blood to write a message.

Find the raven-haired man, or I will be back.

-The Ghost

She knew it was a long shot, but she had to try everything she could. Meloni had to cling to every sliver of hope she had, otherwise she might just have lost all hope from the very start.

She waited until a good amount of the guards were headed to the studio. If it was the Ghost, they had to send more than a handful of men. This made sneaking back up the elevator shaft and into the camp easy. The cooks were nowhere to be seen, but there were multiple loaves of bread and dried meat. Meloni didn't care what sort of meat it was. She gave up caring long ago. When provisions were as scarce as they were in the wasteland, pickiness got people killed.

Pleased with herself and four loaves of bread with enough dried meat to last a week, maybe two, if she was careful, she hastily made her way back to her own home. It was two hours before dusk. She had to be out of sight before the Nighters, and their creatures came. She couldn't fight a horde of them. One or two strays, perhaps, but not a horde.

Thirsty and dying for a drink, she stopped at an oasis, which she knew the exact location of. Meloni made a point not to visit it more often than she should. If her movements could be tracked, she'd be easier to find. It was one of the many lessons she had learned the hard way. She had to learn to fight, to survive, to kill, and to run. She had to learn not to get too attached to people, but she failed the latter miserably. It was impossible to distance oneself from the only family one had. In a world like this, a person clung to every small pleasure they could. They clung to the idea of family, of friends, and being a part of something other than the wasteland. Her attachment was going to get her killed. She knew it, but she had to at least try to save him. Without him, there was nothing left to fight and survive for.

These were the dire thoughts that passed through her mind as she knelt by the small pool of water and filled her bottles. She was playing it dangerously. She hardly had any water left at the camp too.

Lifting her mask to drink, she let the warm liquid soothe her parched throat and lips. She knew only after the chill of the night, there would be cold water. The sun was far too potent for anything to go untouched by its heat.

"Ah, so the Ghost has a face after all," a voice purred from behind her. It was sultry and rough, like nothing she had heard of late. Meloni's heart sped up. How had someone snuck up on her? How was it possible? "People were beginning to think you were one of the Nighters."

Meloni dropped her gear and was on her feet in an instant, the rifle she had picked up aimed at the man's head. It was a stupid weapon to choose. One shot would alert every enemy for miles. The man lazily threw his hands up in the air, and his expression was impossible to see beneath the thick goggles and orange bandana covering his face. An orange bandana; the color of a medic.

She knew better than to lower her weapon. He could

have stolen the bandana anywhere. No one could be trusted.

"Want to maybe switch to a less conspicuous weapon? We don't want to alert the mercs, now do we?"

Meloni lowered her rifle with a huff and quickly switched to a blade that was balanced enough to throw if she had to. She didn't trust this man, and she was grateful that she had that much sense left.

"Who are you?" was all she said.

The man slowly pulled the bandana from his face and pushed his goggles to the top of his head. He was definitely not one of the mercenaries. His eyes were green, the color of moss and emeralds, not the pale blue color of the mercs. "The name's Bryce. I'm a healer from the capital district." That made sense in a way. The capital district often sent healers all over the wasteland to heal stragglers and bring them back to the capital. But why was he alone? Why did her gut feeling tell her that this man was danger-ous? Of course, he was dangerous. Everyone in the waste-land that survived into adulthood was dangerous. Everyone had to fight for survival, even the ones from the capital. "The guards that were sent to guard me got picked up by Nighters. They bought time to escape, but I'm afraid it left me vulnerable to the mercs."

"Why not go back to the capital, then?"

"I became a healer for a reason," he shrugged. "I hate that place; the smell, the people, the power other people have over us. I'd much rather be in the wasteland than back there."

"Then you're just as stupid as the mercs," Meloni shrugged but kept her weapon at the ready. He looked unarmed, but she knew better than anyone that there were places to hide weapons where no one could see. "How did you find me?"

"Find you?" Bryce laughed. "Don't flatter yourself, darling. A man needs to drink. I followed you, yes, but not for the reason you might think. I needed water, and I knew the Ghost was the one who knew the wasteland the best."

"How do you know who I am?"

"Haven't you grown tired of these questions yet?" he sighed. "I was in the encampment when I saw a particular black shadow slip in and out of the kitchen floor. I put two and two together. No one other than the Ghost can slip in and out of a camp unnoticed."

"Except you noticed," she accused, narrowing her eyes.

"It takes a sneak to know a sneak. I was there to gather medical supplies," Bryce said as he held up a container with a faded, red cross. "See?"

"You mean to tell me that you got into the camp in and out unnoticed?"

Bryce looked at his gloved hands as if he was getting bored with this conversation. Tough; she had a lot more questions, questions that needed answers in the wasteland. "I don't mean to brag, but I am a decent climber. I'm good at blending in and getting into places no one else would dare to go."

"A med kit is hardly reason enough to risk your neck."

"We have to be willing to do difficult things, to take chances. Taking risks is how we survive, right?" Meloni hated the fact that he made sense, hated the fact that his story was so believable, but yet her gut still told her otherwise. This man, this man was dangerous.

"Fine, gather some water, then. I won't kill you just yet."

The stranger pulled a face. "But isn't it my turn to ask the questions? That's how a proper exchange works, does it not?"

If he was as dangerous as she could feel he was, she

had to play it safe and go along with his little game. He was much larger than her, and below the layers of clothing, she could tell he was ripped. He had the same build as, as-

She swallowed and nodded for him to continue.

"You're looking for someone," he said with no amount of accusation. It didn't seem like the sort of tone of voice one would use when blackmailing someone. "Who is he?"

"My brother," she confessed.

"Interesting," Bryce pinched his strong chin. "I'll make you a deal, ghostie. I'll pay you double what I pay my own guards, more money than you have probably ever owned to escort me to the next outpost."

"I have no use for your money," she said.

"Perhaps not, but maybe I can keep a look-out for a certain raven-haired man at the outposts. I know the right questions to ask. They trust me, and I am no stranger to buying information. You need my help as much as I need yours."

She hated the fact that he was right. No one would give her any information if she didn't torture it out of them. And if the Scorpion was involved, it would be a death trap. If he had the contacts, the strings to pull, she could use him. But this meant she had to risk her own neck to protect him on the way. She didn't know his skill with weapons, and she wasn't keen on finding out. All she knew was that she needed his help if she was ever going to find her brother.

"Why should I trust you?"

Bryce grinned. "Taking risks is how we survive, remember?"

THREE

A Mushroom Cloud

Meloni hated the heat.

She hated the miserable, bloody heat.

She often dreamed of snow. Of crisp white replacing the beige ocean. She wondered what it must have felt like; living in ice. Meloni often wondered if there were still such places around. Did they hide from her beyond the endless desert? Did they stay far away to mock her, to laugh at her from a distance? It didn't help that she wore the black getup whenever she had a "Ghost" mission. She had an image to maintain, fear to demand from her victims. She was the only one who dared wear black in the desert, and that made her stand out. It made her worthy of being feared.

After patting the stranger down to make sure he had no hidden weapons and examining the med kits to make sure they were legit, only then did she lower her weapon. Only her weapon, not her guard. Never her guard. Lowering one's guard was how you got killed. She still didn't trust him. She didn't think she was ever going to trust him. He was mysterious, and she had no room for mystery in her life. No room for it at all.

When he knelt down for a drink, she stripped down from her grey tank-top and torn beige tights. Layers, she had learned, was a great way to keep the heat out for short periods of time. It was perfect for her ghostly outfit. When she was done, she merely had to strip down and replace her boots and shirt. Then she was just another straggler, trying to survive. From her bag, she pulled brown combat boots that have seen better days and a thin, once white hoodie with a zipper that had turned brown over the years. Her face was the last thing to get covered with a brown bandana. Sunburn was everyone's worst enemy. She couldn't risk it.

"What are you looking at?" She growled as she felt Bryce's eyes on her. She felt it for quite a while now. Felt it ever since she took her black hood off.

"You many have transformed from the Ghost to a mundane human being, but you still lack the charm of the living."

"I have no use for charm," she defended herself.

"And that is why you need a stranger to ask about a brother because you can't do it yourself." He grinned when she looked at him, and she rolled her eyes.

"Can I expect you to be this chatty the entire journey?" Meloni shoved her things back into her backpack, took a swig from her water bottle, and refilled it before shoving that too in the bag.

"Oh, yes," Bryce said, his grin still wide and goofy. It made Meloni wonder what his past was like. She wished she could smile like that. If only she didn't have the ghost of herself inside of her where a living, beating heart should have been.

"Do I have to listen and pretend to be interested?"

Bryce filled his own water bottle and got to his feet as he shrugged. "It's part of the job description."

"I'm starting to regret taking this job," was all she mumbled before heading North, toward the nearest outpost.

"Oh, I can't be that bad. I'm handsome, I'm funny, and I'm good in-"

"I don't want to hear it," she said as she interrupted him. She didn't want him to think that there was going to be any form of small-talk. Talking meant getting to know each other, and the more he got to know her, the more weaknesses he would find to hold against her later. Besides, she had worse things to think about. Like nightfall being upon them. She stopped in her tracks. She completely forgot about nightfall. One look in his direction, and she could tell he thought the same. They needed shelter from the night terrors.

"I don't suppose you have a shack in that rucksack of yours?" he asked rhetorically, and Meloni huffed. She regretted what she was about to say even before saying it.

"We'll have to head to my place. It's North East, toward the capital." Taking the compass from her pocket, she turned to face North East, fighting the gut-wrenching realization. She had to move when this was all over. He knew who she was, where she lived. This was going to complicate things. But there was no other choice. It was this or suffer at the hands of the Nighters.

"Your place? Well, usually, I have to buy a lady dinner first, but if you insist." Meloni's nostrils flared as she turned on him. He took a step back.

"Listen here and listen carefully. I don't trust you, and the fact that I am giving up my haven that I have been safe in since I was a child isn't supposed to be a joke to you. None of this is funny. This world isn't funny, this situation isn't funny, and that smile on your face is not charming. It's infuriating, and I want nothing more than to smack it off your face. I am desperate here, and you are not making my situation any less difficult so if you-"

There was a blast in the distance, and Meloni ducked, covering her head with her hands. There was another blow, louder this time. Bombs... They were bombs.

"Shit," Bryce cursed as he pushed his hood from his head, revealing blond hair. Meloni was sure it would have been platinum if it wasn't for the dirt and sand. She followed his gaze after recovering from the near heart attack. She saw the remnants of a mushroom cloud in the direction of the encampment she infiltrated earlier, though it was impossible to tell which one the bomb hit. There were a bunch of camps in that general direction, and all of them had some sort of beef with the other. It was just another casualty in a war among the many factions of the ravaged world. Who blew up who, she didn't really know or necessarily care, but Bryce obviously did.

"What is it?"

"That was where we were headed."

Meloni watched the black smoke reach the heavens, a sign that there was a fire that no one had yet extinguished. "Fuck."

FOUR

Desperate Times

MELONI'S HOME WAS TUCKED INTO THE GROUND JUST outside of the capital.

The capital was built from scrap metal and wood that survived. Although it was tearing away little by little, they always managed to keep the fifty-foot wall in mint condition. The wall was thick, about seven feet of corrugated iron. This meant that there were a lot of hollow parts here and there. Perfect for a safe house. Meloni had only briefly seen the inside of the capital and swore never to return. Containers were stacked atop one another, and makeshift apartments forced five to ten people into one container depending on the wealth of the citizens. The higher-class citizens had the highest containers that overlooked the city and wasteland below. Meloni doubted they had to share.

Her brother grew up in the capital, and when she was born, he took her away. He didn't want her to grow up the same way he did. At the mercy of the wealthy. So, he found a little square in the walls, and it was where she grew up. No one ever found them. No one ever thought to look inside the walls. They managed to connect their little abode to the power source. It wasn't much, but it was home.

After years of the corroded iron surrounding them, they fell ill and had to find a new home. They didn't want to move away from the capital. They were safe there, being guarded at night from the Nighters and were kept safe from the mercs that dared attack the capital. It was the perfect place for them. There was power, security.

Then one day, by chance, Meloni stumbled upon a latch while she was scavenging the outskirts of the wall for scraps to eat. It was hidden beneath a pile of scrap, and she had to call her brother to help her open it.

Inside, they found a little room stacked with provisions and luxuries that they could never afford elsewhere. Even the walls were free of corrosion. It was pure luck that they found the bunker so close to the capital. Meloni remembered that she thought the gods hadn't forsaken them completely after all.

The bunker was small, made for one person alone, so they had to improvise. Instead of full beds, they scavenged mattresses. They pushed them against opposite walls with blankets and pillows to give the illusion of comfort. Meloni tried her best to make the little hole in the wall a home. She often brought home books or posters to provide the place with a bit of life. She even grabbed some fairy lights from an old house she raided a few years ago. Only half the room was still standing, the rest seemingly burned away as the edges of the walls were singed black. A few of the globes were missing now, but the few that still worked gave the room a cozy ambiance. An ambiance that was soon to be invaded by a stranger. She was tempted to tell him that the deal was off, that he could not join her in her little home. Wasn't he a resident of the capital? Why didn't he offer her a place to stay for the night? She wanted to believe that he was genuine, she really did. She wanted at least one person she could trust as much as she trusted her brother. It would be nice, she thought.

"You live in the capital?" Her companion's voice was soft next to her, and she fought the urge to jump. Not many people had the ability to sneak up on her, and it didn't help that this individual was who he was.

"Not in the capital, per se," she said as she approached the side of the wall. The usual shift was on duty, the one guard that loved them like siblings. Carter smiled at her as they approached, then narrowed his eyes at the medic at her side. If Bryce was shocked at the friendly meeting, his body language didn't say as much. The man was as solid and composed as a sculpture.

"I didn't think you were bringing company," was all Carter said before Bryce snaked himself around Meloni to shake the guard's hand. They exchanged a look that Meloni didn't care for. "Medic," Carter started. "I wasn't informed that we had any medics on patrol today."

Meloni shot Bryce a look. She knew it, she bloody knew it. "That's because I was supposed to return four weeks ago."

"I don't blame you for staying away as long as you possibly can," Carter nodded in understanding. "Things are getting pretty rough in there. Still, the commander is probably looking for you."

"I doubt it," Bryce shrugged. "I faked my death three days into the expedition."

"Then why still medic your way through the waste-land?" Meloni couldn't help herself. Things were starting to make more sense to her.

He was so sly because he was used to evading the offi-cials. He didn't offer her a place to stay because, as soon as they saw his face in the capital, they would most likely execute him.

"I joined the medics not only because I wanted to see the wasteland, Ghostie. I want to help people. The people who don't have anyone to help them." Meloni cringed at the nickname but realized that she hadn't given him her name yet. Neither had he asked. He was respecting her privacy.

"Well," Carter started, looking over his shoulder at the patrol rounding the corner. "You better get a move on if you want to make it to the Hole in time. I might be able to get you out of a pinch, but I'm not so sure about him." He pointed at Bryce, who nodded in understanding, although his face furrowed at the mention of a hole.

"We'll be out of sight in no time," Meloni reassured and kissed him on the cheek before grabbing Bryce by the elbow and pulling him in the opposite direction.

"Hey Mel," Carter said, as a bit of an afterthought. Her heart sank to her stomach. She knew what he was going to ask. She knew it from the tone of his voice, the desperate tone that only came with the loss of a brother. It was the tone she too carried whenever she spoke of him. Meloni turned on her heels. Bryce had the mind to walk away from them slightly, giving them privacy.

"Any news?"

Meloni stepped closer to Carter. "No news," she said and pointed to her companion. "But he might have more access to information. I'm hoping to uncover some things within the next day or two."

"He's lucky to have a sister like you." Carter pulled her into a tight bear hug. As sweet as it looked from the outside, it was all a ploy to whisper in her ear. "I don't trust that bloke. I have never seen him in my life. Sleep with one eye open and your hand on the radio."

Meloni swallowed hard and nodded. "I know he's not who he says he is. But he does have contacts and ways of getting information. No one knows anything, and the Scorpion has been mentioned multiple times."

"The Scorpion, Mel, come on. Would he really want you to go up against the Scorpion?" Carter held her at arms-length now. Her nostrils flared.

"He would go up against the capital for both of us, and you know it." Meloni's words were hissed through clenched teeth.

Slowly, Carter tugged at the necklace around her neck, pulling it from her shirt and holding it in front of her face. "If your brother was taken by the Scorpion and you go after him, this will be all that's left of both of you."

Meloni ripped the dog tags from his hands. "I'd rather be nothing together than something apart."

Without another word, she turned around. She strode toward Bryce with the swagger she usually wore as the Ghost, trying to hide the fact that she was dying on the inside. That she wanted to scream and curse at the world. She wanted to yell at the heavens and ask why it took him. Why it took her beloved brother.

In the dim, dusk light, she could see Bryce eyeing her. She growled at him, not stopping or motioning for him to follow. He followed anyway. "What?"

"You're different with him than with me."

Meloni snorted. "He didn't lie to me about being a medic for the capital."

"Technically, it wasn't as much a lie as it was stretching the truth."

Meloni sighed and looked at him, defeat stretched across her face. It was the first time she allowed herself to show on her face what she felt in her heart. Meloni was no closer to finding her brother, and her only hope relied on a liar that may or may not be who he said he was. She was exhausted, and the only thing she wanted was to sleep the desperation away. Meloni found that sleep was the best way to get rid of it, and she woke up every day feeling refreshed with a new sense of determination. It was time for that sleep now, but it was going to be difficult sharing a space with this man that she did not trust as far as she could throw him.

"Listen, Bryce, I am tired. You lied about who and what you are, and there is no way around it. You are trying to play with words, and I grew up with someone who used to trick me into doing all kinds of things, and I can tell a lie from a truth a mile away. I still don't believe your story, and the only reason I am entertaining you is because I am really damn desperate. So please, for the love of everything good in the world, keep your mouth shut!" Her outburst fell on deaf ears as he focused on something behind her. He pulled her close to him before pushing her against the wall, towering over her. He cocooned her between himself and the metal wall.

She hissed, but he shushed her.

Then she heard it; a car. There were voices of three, no four men, and the music was loud. Bryce leaned in closer to her, and she realized what he was doing. To the untrained eye, they were merely two, horny civilians who couldn't get enough of each other.

She looked up at him. Still, his eyes were in the corners of his eyes, relying on his peripheral vision to warn them if anyone came closer. His orange bandana around his neck caught her attention. She remembered Carter saying that they didn't expect a medic outside the walls today. With the sun setting at a rapid pace, she doubted anyone would notice the cloth, but she wrapped her arms around his neck anyway. If he was shocked, he didn't let his body show as much. Instead, he leaned in closer, their noses touching. She could hardly breathe. Not because of sparks that flew above their heads or an undying need to have him, but because she had never been so intimate with another human being. She wasn't used to the closeness, the smell of her scent mingling with someone else's. It was nice.

Whistles echoed as the car drove by, a nonchalant warning that it was nearly curfew, and they wouldn't want to be outside when the Nighters came. Bryce pulled away from Meloni, and the smirk he gave the passing men was infuriating. She wanted to kick him in the crotch then and there. But she didn't; instead, she let him lower his head toward hers again and wondered what it would have been like to be kissed. Not by him, not by anyone in particular. Just to be kissed like a normal girl while breaking curfew. Just to be kissed like she had never been kissed before, without the weight of survival on her shoulders.

She sighed when he pulled away, followed by a deep breath. It was for one moment. She allowed herself that one moment, but it was over now. It was back to surviving now.

"This way," her voice was raspy as she jogged out in front of him. She felt him follow her. She didn't hear him; she didn't hear a single step he took. It was his presence that made her jog faster.

At the back end of the capital's wall, Meloni side-stepped a particularly large pile of trash before finding the loose steel sheet that hid the latch to her home. She looked at him, then at the latch, and opened it just as the sun had fully set, and the moon graced them with her presence.

She was letting a stranger into her home. She only hoped that it was not a big mistake.

FIVE

Sleepless Nights

WHEN SHE LED HIM INTO THE BUNKER, HE WAS QUIET AT first, taking in the scenery around him. She knew that look, the way he took everything in. He wanted to know where the weapons were, what he could use to his advantage if he had to escape. It was the same way she scanned a room once she entered it, and it made her feel uneasy. She knows how deadly she was with her bare hands, and if this man, this towering, muscled man found so much as a single knife, she was doomed. She was completely and utterly doomed. She couldn't fight him. If she used her small size to her advantage, she might have a chance of escaping but nothing more. He had the upper hand, and in some weird, abnormal way, she knew that he knew that. He did not make a move to attack her though, and that meant that he needed her. That was good. As long as they could be useful to one another, neither would get killed.

She shared her bread and dried meat with him, and they ate in silence. They didn't talk, didn't make eye contact. They didn't say anything after the intimate scene against the wall. She was embarrassed. Embarrassed because she got carried away by the scene and he, well, perhaps he was just over it. Maybe his fascination with her ended as soon as he found out that she was indeed human under her ghostly façade. She didn't know why she cared. She didn't care… She didn't.

After dinner, they washed up in the small basin of the makeshift bathroom. Carter connected the water from the capital to the bunker somehow. It wasn't heated, but the cold water was refreshing after the scorching hot days. Meloni gave him some of her brother's clothes, which proved to be a little tight around the chest, so he opted to go bare-chested instead. It was a glorious sight. A sight she tried to avoid with every glance. He smirked at her whenever he caught her looking at him, and her nostrils flared every time. Not because she was mad at him, but because she was angry at herself for looking. Stupid female hormones. They really did choose an inconvenient time to present themselves to her. She had never been attracted to anyone, not really. And she wasn't sure what to make of it.

Surely she could find the man attractive and suspicious at the same time. Surely she could hate being around him and fantasize about his chest.

Only, she found that she didn't hate him. He was funny and charming. He was helpful when they were cleaning up the table, and he thanked her for the clothes. He was smart and good looking. The only reason she didn't fall head over heels was that he was a liar. He was a filthy, rotting liar. If only she knew what he was lying about.

He also had a scar beneath the bandana around his neck. It was an ugly gash that looked like something that should have killed the person sporting it. It made her even more suspicious of him. If he were a medic, no one would have wanted to kill him. Doctors were too valuable and scarce. None of it made sense. He made no sense, and it drove her mad. It drove her absolutely crazy. She was used to getting her way, and now she wasn't getting it. She knew that he was going to betray her the first chance he got, but she had no proof. He had given her no proof to confirm her theories. Now she merely sounded like a madwoman determined to make him the villain.

After washing up, she led him to her brother's bed, where he nonchalantly fell onto the mattress and stretched out his long, muscled legs. He still wore his socks even in this heat. That was how a person knew the other was a psychopath. No person in their right mind went to bed while wearing socks.

Meloni trudged to her own mattress and nestled into the blankets. Nights were getting colder, which meant winter was close. Provisions were going to get scarce very soon. She sighed.

"So," Bryce said with a sigh. She looked at him, but he didn't look at her. Only stared at the fused fairy lights overhead. "Your name is Mel?"

Meloni shrugged. "Actually, it's Meloni."

"You don't like the abbreviation?"

"I don't like it when people know my name in general," she admitted. "I like to keep it to myself as long as I can."

"Why?"

Meloni sighed. "The more people know my name, the more likely my identity will be revealed. My livelihood depends on people thinking that I am some sort of inhuman creature that has to hide her face because of how hideous she is. If people believe I was just a girl-" her voice trailed off.

"Then they will know that you have weaknesses," he said, finishing her sentence. She nodded as she watched the lights above her own head. One of the bulbs was blinking. It was going to die soon.

"Your brother, what's his name?" he inquired.

"Why do you want to know?"

Bryce sighed. "Because it will be easier to find him if I know his name."

It was Meloni's chance to sigh. "Michael," she said. "But he's better known as the Smuggler."

There was a hearty laugh that rumbled from Bryce's chest, and she looked at him with an accusatory glare. "I should have known the infamous Smuggler and deadly Ghost were related." There was a moment of silence and then: "How did he get taken?"

"Yes, well, many people didn't like this dynamic duo thing we had going on, so they set up a trap. It was flawless. Even now, I can't see through it. Someone hired us to do a job, and then, in the middle of the wasteland, an army of men rose from the sand. They knew the route we were going to take, and they took advantage of that. Michael knew something was off, though. I don't know how he knew, but he did. He even gave me his dog-tags and made me promise that I would run if anything happened. Like a coward, I actually did."

"I don't think you were a coward," Bryce said softly.

Meloni found herself close to tears, but she wiped at her eyes, concealing it as a scratch. A well of emotion threatened to overflow, and she wasn't ready for it. "Then, what was I?"

There was a rustle that came from the medic, and when she looked his way, he had turned on his side to look at her. "I think that you were afraid, and you acted the same way any rational person would. You're honest and loyal. Of course, you were going to keep your promise and run. I think that you did the smart thing because if you were both captured, who would go looking for you? That bitch ass guard? Please? He'd shit himself the first Nighter he sees."

Meloni snorted. "Carter thinks things through a million times before actually doing it. He would weigh out the pros and cons of saving us first, then act accordingly. I don't know. I guess I'm just frustrated that I hadn't found him in the month that he's been gone. Now I'm starting to believe that the Scorpion might have something to do with it, and that scares me." She cringed when she realized what she had admitted to a complete stranger. But who was he going to tell? If he was going to take her down, he was going to do so anyway. Perhaps it was a good idea for her to unload her problems a little. Not just on herself, but to someone else.

"The Scorpion has nothing to do with it," Bryce said, and she frowned.

"How do you know?"

"Seriously?" he raised an eyebrow. "It's not his style. Sure, he can be brutal at times, but he wouldn't be stupid enough to piss off the Ghost. I'd like to think he's smarter than that."

"You have really high respect for him, don't you?"

"No, I just know that he doesn't deal with people unless they spoiled his plans directly. You didn't steal from him or kill his people, did you?"

Meloni shook her head. "We tried to stick with the low-ranking mercs. We didn't want trouble with someone that had the potential of killing us."

"And there you have it. Say what you want about the Scorpion, but he does have some sense of honor, I think."

"What about being the most notoriously dangerous and brutal mercenary makes you think that he has honor?" Meloni didn't want to accept that the Scorpion might not have Michael. That would mean she was exactly back where she started. With no information, no leads. She had to believe that she at least had something. At least thinking that the Scorpion took him gave her someone to blame. It gave her something to focus on and to hate.

"The same thing that made me believe the Ghost actually had a heart. I'm smart like that." Bryce turned back to watch the roof of the bunker, and she could faintly hear the growls of Nighters above them. They must have been desperate if they were risking getting this close to the capital. She knew that Bryce was thinking the same thing without having to look at him.

They stayed like that for a while, just listening to the Nighters above them, scavenging for food. A gunshot rang in the distance, and a guard must have seen one. Most of the growling quieted after that. They must have fled.

Falling asleep became an impossible task for Meloni. Not only did her houseguest snore like a grizzly bear, but he also carried the distinctive scent of lies on his clothes.

So, her night was spent thrashing and turning. Watching the medic sleep as she contemplated the events of the day that had passed. As well as what was to follow.

Firstly, she made a mental list of the things she knew for a fact.

She knew that her brother was taken and that she had to find him. She knew that she had a skilled companion to aid her on this quest, but Meloni didn't know how much she could trust him. Perhaps he would give her location away to the same people who took her brother. And finally, she knew that the Scorpion didn't have Michael. She didn't know how she could tell, but she just could. It was something in the way that the medic said it that made her believe it. She believed that the Scorpion wouldn't stoop so low as to take the life of someone who didn't cross him. But what if Michael did? What if he got into some bad business without her knowing, and it made the Scorpion angry? Still, she just had a feeling that the Scorpion didn't have Michael. She could feel it in her bones.

Next, Meloni went over the things that could very possibly happen the next day.

They were going to an outpost, and Bryce would find something about Michael. Some clue that point in a general direction. Would they split paths then? Would he accompany her on the rescue mission? Somehow she doubted that he would leave her to her own devices. She may not have trusted him. Still, there was something about him that told her that he might not be telling the full truth, but he did have a little honor beneath that cocky grin and nonchalant attitude.

Bryce gave a particularly loud snore, and Meloni cringed. Even if the butterflies in her stomach died down, there was no sleeping on her part going to happen. Not while she was in the same room as that beast.

It was going to be a long, long night.

SIX

The Beginning of the Journey

MELONI HAD BEEN CONTEMPLATING HER OPTIONS FOR A good ten minutes, and she was starting to get on her own nerves.

After a night with little to no sleep, and then being jolted awake when she finally did drift off by a cheery whistle, Meloni was not feeling up for the day. If she didn't have enough reason not to trust this man, she sure did now. Who the hell was this cheery in the morning? When she and Michael woke up, it usually took about an hour for them to even speak to each other. This was unnatural.

Her head pounded as if she had drunk too much the previous night. If only it was that and not a complete assessment of her own life. Her mind had been reeling all night, and she didn't know what to make of it. All that thinking, all that plotting, and she was still no further in figuring anything out.

She watched as he tied his shoelaces; tightly and a little too perfect for a normal human being. Meloni shook her head. She was being an idiot, of course. Her lack of sleep had made her even more skeptical of this man. Was that a good or a bad thing, though? Would it help her in the days to come on their journey? She doubted it. It only made her more paranoid.

She shifted her gaze at the collection of weapons on the makeshift dining room table again and cringed. She couldn't leave Bryce defenseless, but she couldn't give him a weapon either. She had Michael's extra weapons shoved in her rucksack. Deciding that her life was more valuable than him being able to defend himself, she strapped the rest of her weapons and guns onto her body, then extracted her brother's second pistol from the bag and tucked that into the back of her pants instead. Rather safe than sorry. If things went south, with him or on the road with mercenaries, she had to be able to defend herself. She had to be sure she had enough gun power and blades to cut through an army. Only then was she satisfied enough to drape her beige cloak over her shoulders and shove her ghost outfit into the bag. She looked back at the doctor and found him looking at her with a raised eyebrow.

"And here I thought we had a bonding moment last night," was all he said as he got to his feet from the bed he occupied. His long legs looking twice as long after the outfit change. His cargo pants were fitted. Not tight enough to be constricting, but not loose enough to take away from the shape of his hips and thighs. His t-shirt was ripped at the lower seam, but it didn't distract from the low V-shape the collar made, his smooth chest peeking out, teasing whoever looked its way. His shoulders were broad, and she knew it was partially because he squared them with the confidence he had. The man basically oozed self-assurance, and it showed in the way he carried himself. It was different than the sneaky swagger Meloni had. This was out-there and noticeable from a mile away. This man knew he was good looking, smart, and probably as deadly with those healer's hands as he was good with a bandage. That, of course, was only the case if he actually was a healer.

Bryce's face was covered in a light brown stubble. Instead of having the spaghetti strainer patches her brother sported from time to time, she could tell his was even and full. For the first time since they met, she wondered how old he was. He couldn't have been much older than twenty-eight, surely. He had no wrinkles and no scars except the nasty gash on his neck that she found her eyes returning to time and time again. His green eyes danced with mischief.

Meloni growled. "That was before you started snoring like a grizzly bear and kept me up all night," she accused.

"I do not snore, thank you very much," he said and approached the small table where he had discarded his pack and medical supplies upon arriving. He pulled his own cloak from the sack and draped it over his shoulders.

Meloni huffed and moved to the basin so she could wash her face and hands one last time before heading out into the desert for an uncertain amount of time. She caught a glimpse of herself in the mirror. Thick, raven black hair pulled into a tight ponytail, dark, thick eyelashes, sun-kissed skin that was still paler than most people in the wasteland. All of these things seemed normal to her... All of it except...

She had dark circles beneath her navy-blue eyes. She gasped and turned to the medic, and accusation written on her face. He didn't look at her, though. Instead, he was looking at something else. A photo... He shoved it in his pants pocket quickly, and Meloni averted her gaze. That was one of the secrets... That was a clue to who he really was. Meloni would never be able to get that photograph, but it did prove that he was hiding something.

Why be so secretive with something that he didn't have to hide?

"Are you going to tell me which outpost we're going to?" Meloni asked as a way to break the silence.

"Nope," he said, no trace of lingering emotion in his voice. "Just follow and protect me."

"I have no doubt that you don't need my protection." Her words were out before she could stop herself. They looked at each other for a second, and then he grinned.

"Maybe I just want a companion. Life can get lonely on the road as I am sure you know."

"Yes," she admitted. "That's the way I like it."

Bryce tilted his head to the side as if seeing a side of her that he hadn't considered before. Meloni felt exposed, as if he could see through her clothing, through her skin and bones and into her soul. "Do you really mean that, or is it something you tell yourself to feel better about your situation?"

Meloni opened her mouth to retort, but she couldn't find the words.

Was she really that transparent? Did he see all that just by looking at her? She wasn't even sure that what he was saying about her was true and yet... And yet it pulled at her emotional strings, and she didn't like it. She didn't like learning things about herself through the grapevine.

"How long will we be on the road?" She had to change the subject; she had to somehow shift the topic from her to something else entirely.

Bryce shrugged. "Hard to say. A few days. Five at most."

Meloni sighed. That was what she was afraid of. They'd have to find shelter somewhere. No tent was safe against the Nighters, so they had to rely on finding old buildings they could hide in during the nights. She hated long expeditions. She much preferred raiding the outposts close to the capital. It was easier, safer, a guaranteed win for her. This was going to be one hell of a trip.

AN HOUR LATER, they were on their way, sleeping bags strapped to their packs and enough dried meat to feed a pack of sand wolves. Meloni shivered at the thought. She had only heard of such creatures but never traveled far enough to find them.

It was said that the elements changed their fur. They no longer had the furry tails or bushy manes... No, their skin was like leather and twice as durable. Only a bullet to the head could stop them. Meloni's aim wasn't nearly as good as Michael's, and she doubted she'd be able to shoot it if push came to shove. She preferred knives. They were easier to wield and somehow felt more intimate. It was easier to take a life that way. In her mind, people, no matter who they were, deserved an intimate death. Not a cold, hard bullet to the heart. That wasn't her style. She hoped they wouldn't encounter sand wolves.

She followed Bryce North. The sun was already baking her like a poached egg. In all the years of evolution, humanity went through after the Great War; they still weren't immune to the heat. They did not adapt like the animals did. She wished she had leathery skin that the heat bounced off of. She wished that she had somewhere down the line grew hooves so she could walk better in the sand instead of sinking into it with every step she took. She could already feel her boots fill up with sand. Just another day in the wasteland.

"Remind me again why I agreed to do this?" Meloni didn't bother hiding the bitterness in her voice. This was not a good day for her, the worst she's had in a long, long while.

The doctor stopped and pulled his bandana from his face. He didn't wear his goggles, and the sand had turned the whites of his eyes red. It made his green eyes pop.

After pulling his water bottle from his pack, he offered her a sip, which she refused, and took a sip himself. "Well, Ghostie, because I am just that irresistible."

Meloni chuckled. "Do you ever get tired of the façade?"

He raised an eyebrow. "What façade?"

Motioning in his general direction, Meloni pulled her own water from her pack and took a sip. She didn't trust his water either. "This," she said. "You."

"Meloni, I am not a façade. I may be more than I appear to be on the outside, but I am who I am. I never lied about that."

"So, you admit that you are hiding things from me?"

Bryce chuckled. "You mean to tell me that you have told me the entire truth? Have you shared your entire backstory with a complete stranger? I'm not much of a narrator, but I told you the things about me that you needed to know. You know I'm a doctor, you know that my guards were killed, and you know that I am not afraid of taking risks. You know I am a skilled climber, and I know that you didn't give me any weapons because you can tell I'm a skilled fighter too. What else do you want to know?"

Meloni chewed on his answer for a bit. It was the truth. It was all she really needed to know, but she found herself wanting to know more. It wasn't an infatuation. That would be ridiculous. It was merely a fascination, and she was angry that he didn't share things voluntarily when he clearly had the upper hand. "Where is your family?"

"Where is yours?" His question confused her.

"My brother is taken, remember?"

"Not him," he shook his head before turning his back on her and looking into the distance. "Someone must have birthed you."

Her mother. She never spoke of her, never wanted to. She was an evil woman who was addicted to morphine most of her life. Michael took her away from that, from her life. She hardly remembered her mother, but she did remember this; needles and the smell of medicine. "I don't know where my parents are," Meloni confessed. Perhaps if she shared something about herself, he would return the favor.

"I don't have any. They died a long time ago." There was a melancholy tone to his voice, and it made her sad. Was that the picture he was looking at earlier? Was it of his parents, his siblings? She wanted to say that she was sorry, but she knew that those words held no weight whatsoever. They were words someone spoke when they had no idea how to respond. Instead, she asked another question.

"Where are we going?"

Bryce sighed. "The Barracks."

SEVEN

Second Thoughts

THE BARRACKS...

Meloni swallowed, her mouth dry.

It was the camp with the largest military force in the new world. They were the cut-throat mercenaries that answered to one man alone; the Scorpion. There was no way that she was going there. She couldn't. She would risk her neck for a fool's errand. Their security was nothing like the capital's. There was no sneaking around undetected. She didn't know the layout, the guards, or the formations. Didn't know which structures were safe and which weren't. She had hoped he wanted to go to a camp she knew. One where she was familiar with the layout and guard routines. The amount of time it would take to figure out where she could get in and out would finish their resources. It could take days, weeks even. What the hell was he thinking? Was he suicidal?

"The Barracks? Did I hear you correctly, or do I have a sand snake in my ear?"

"All I need is to get there. I have a way in. Trust me."

"Trust you?" she laughed. "You are leading us into a death trap, and I am supposed to trust you?"

"Listen, if anyone knows anything about your brother, that person will be in the Barracks," there was a tone of annoyance in his voice that she didn't enjoy. "I am not an idiot, Meloni."

It was the first time he used her name, and it felt odd, in a way. Foreign, even. How dare he? How dare he do this to her? He was putting her in more danger than she had ever put herself in. If she didn't ask, she wasn't going to find out where they were going until they arrived.

Meloni started walking in the direction she came from, dead set on going home.

"Where are you going?" Bryce asked from his spot in the dune. He didn't move to follow her, and she didn't stop either.

"Home," she said simply. "To a place I won't get killed."

"Oh, please," the doctor huffed. "You are safer in the wasteland than in that underground tin can."

Meloni's nostrils flared, and she spun around. But when she turned around, her eye caught a glimmer in the distance. She told him to duck a millisecond before the gunshot went off.

The doctor had quick reflexes, and he ducked a moment before the bullet zoomed over them. Meloni fell to the ground, her mouth filled with sand. She spat.

"An ambush," he hissed. "We'll have to fight our way out of this."

Bryce barely finished his sentence before he was pulled off the ground by two men half his size. They were short and stubby, but she had no illusion about their strength. Size didn't matter for the bandits. Their endurance and pain tolerance made up for their weakness sevenfold.

In awe, she watched as he took on both of them, pulling his arms free from their grip, turning around to face them, and smashing their heads together. They crumpled to the sand simultaneously. She had never seen anything like it. His brute strength, the speed at which he moved, was incredible. She was certain she could watch him dance around the bandits all day, smashing their heads in and growling animalistically at anyone who dared challenge him.

She was sure she could, but Meloni knew she shouldn't. She had to get up and fight for her own survival. Bryce had lost his pack somewhere in the chaos as four more men appeared behind him. They were emerging from the North, then. Meloni slithered from beneath her pack, leaving it exactly where she was lying. They hadn't seen her yet. That was good. She always did rely on the element of surprise. Another gunshot rang from the same spot as before. She knew the sniper had to be taken out. He was the most dangerous weapon in the bandit's arsenal at the moment.

Crawling across the sand, half-sunken into the hot ground, she pulled a knife from her thigh and kept it between her teeth. Closer and closer, she crawled to the fighting. Bryce had his hands full, and as strong as he was, she could tell taking on five of them was taking a toll on him. She had to step in soon, or he was sure to be dead.

She entertained the thought for a moment. Thought about it, then decided against it. Bryce was a valuable ally. Perhaps if she saved his ass, he would see reason and tell her not to go with him. Maybe he'll understand her reluctance better. Maybe he would go on alone and still ask about her brother when he got to the camp. Keeping him alive would benefit her more than having him killed.

She reached the chaos, and once she was close enough,

she pushed herself onto her haunches and struck like a viper. Her blade in her hand, she was a deadly cyclone that demanded blood. The bandits didn't even have time to finish their battle cry by the time she cut down three bandits. The other two paused and took a step back. Bryce grinned at them like a maniac. He was enjoying the fight. He was enjoying the crunch of bone when his fist collided with their ribs. He enjoyed watching the blood drip from their mouths and the painful sting of sand in his busted knuckles.

"I'm going after the sniper," she said casually, dropping down to her haunches again. The doctor nodded that he heard her as he punched one of the bandits in the throat and kicked another in the stomach. Two more were approaching, and she knew that he could handle them. The sniper was her priority.

Sneaking over to where she saw the glint of sun on the scope was easy. There were enough dunes to hide behind, and her smart color choice meant that she blended well with the wasteland. With the sniper occupied and shooting at the doctor, who he skillfully dodged every time and had the mind not to stand still, she made it to his location without as much as a hitch. It was almost too easy. Almost as if it was a trap.

Meloni gasped at the realization, but it was too late. Two men and a woman already circled her when she got to the dune the sniper was hiding behind. The sniper was a lanky woman who didn't have the sort of face you'd wish upon your worst enemy.

Meloni took a deep breath, called the Ghost inside her, and moved like the wraith she was. Her movements were smooth and graceful, and her blade met flesh with every swing. She didn't miss. Not once. One body fell with a gurgle, the other with a groan, and soon she was only left with the sniper who had the rifle aimed at her head. She could see the red dot move over her face. When it settled on her forehead, a wave of fear washed over Meloni.

Everything happened too fast. She hardly had time to register the fighting. She could barely recall killing any of the bandits.

This was not the way she was supposed to die. She always imagined her death being a noble one. One where she had saved a camp of slaves from a ruthless mercenary lord with her brother by her side and maybe a rocking tune playing from a car radio somewhere nearby.

Meloni closed her eyes and said a quick prayer, apologizing to Michael that she couldn't get to him in time.

Then there was a battle cry. It was feral and rough. Like someone had amputated a man's leg with anesthesia. Meloni opened her eyes and found the doctor midair, lunging toward the sniper. There was a satisfying crunch when his elbow hit her ribs, and she fell to the sand with a gasp. Had he taken care of the bandits that fast? It must have been only a minute after she arrived at the sniper's hiding spot. He still had to make his way across the dunes to get to her. Just how skilled of a fighter was this man?

No sound escaped her throat as she opened her mouth wide in a silent scream. Meloni would have screamed too if Bryce's face was the one above hers, his fist flying and his temper on display. Meloni didn't stop him. She knew she should have, but she didn't. Letting the sniper live was more dangerous than any sand wolf. She could lead people to them. She could gather an army to march on them. They couldn't leave a single loose end. This was the sad reality of the wasteland. There was no mercy, not unless you wanted to get killed.

Bryce ended it with a final punch.

He had beaten her to death. In fact, he had beaten them all to death…

He had no weapon aside from his fists, and he took down double the amount of men she did. The doctor was a killing machine, and Meloni found it unsettling. Could a doctor really do that to another human being? Wasn't it a doctor's motto to help people? If he was a doctor, what did that say about him?

Meloni shook the negative thoughts from her head.

It meant that he wanted to survive. He was willing to do anything to survive, and he had saved her life doing it.

Bryce got to his feet and looked at her, the feral spark that was in his eyes a moment ago had vanished into thin air. She was unsure whether it was the unbearable heat or the sight that had stolen her breath. It was a magnificent sight. It was terrible and scary and oh so impressive.

He lost his cloak along the way, and there was a triangle of sweat on his chest. The bandana was also lost along somewhere. The brutal scar on his neck made more prominent by his bulging veins and redness.

"You saved me," was all she could say. She didn't know what else she could say. She didn't know if a 'thank you' was in order. The only person who ever risked his life for her was Michael. She had never met anyone else willing to do it; never mind a stranger. Bryce smiled at her.

"You can pay me back by being my bodyguard on the trip to the Barracks."

Meloni croaked out a laugh. Unbelievable, he was unbelievable. "You don't need a bodyguard."

Bryce shrugged, wiping his sweaty face with his shirt. It exposed his muscled abdomen. "Perhaps not. But I could use the company of a pretty girl who can hold her own in a fight."

Pretty girl… "So, I'm an accessory?"

The doctor considered it for a moment. "Yes, but you have a use. You're not just for show. It's why I'm attracted to you."

"You're attracted to me? We've known each other a day." Meloni couldn't believe what she was hearing. It was madness.

"Attraction isn't love, Meloni. You are allowed to be attracted to a person you only just met or even just admired from a distance. Honestly, any man who isn't attracted to you is either attracted to the same sex or family," Bryce shrugged. Meloni tried to hide a blush behind wiping her face with her cloak. "Besides, that warm, charming personality had me at the get-go," his words dripped with sarcasm, and Meloni chuckled.

"It's the looks that attract them and the personality that keeps them." She couldn't remember the last time she had a pleasant exchange with someone. This was nice. Perhaps she was being a little harsh on him. Perhaps she could do this thing and go with him to the Barracks. Perhaps she could warm up to him a little. He was definitely a useful ally, and it helped that he was easy on the eye. He was a good companion until she had Michael back. She wasn't sure what would happen after that, and she didn't allow herself to think past that point. Thinking too far ahead made a person lose track of the present.

Bryce chuckled. "Why do you think I saved you?" He looked toward the dune where their packs were, then back at Meloni. "Let's find shelter for the night. I'm starving, and I don't think I have a lot more miles in me. Those bastards really did a number on my ribs."

EIGHT

Angels or Balls of Gas?

It was night. The two companions sat in contempt silence, staring at the star-speckled sky. The Nighters howled in the distance. Although the night was cold, they did not start a fire. Any sign of life assured an attack from the Nighters. Even with their combined skills, they were no match for them. So, they wrapped themselves in their cloaks and sat close together. It felt strangely familiar even though they didn't talk. Even though there were layers and layers of clothing between them, it was the most intimate thing Meloni had ever experienced.

Was this friendship? Were they friends?

She tried to think about when she was a child in the capital. She tried to think about friends she might have had but she couldn't. She remembered trying to make friends with the other children, but none of them really bothered returning her enthusiasm. She was weird, more interested in combat tactics than playing tag. If she were anyone but herself, she probably wouldn't have wanted to be friends with herself either.

As a teenager, she only had her brother. When Carter

discovered their Hole, he became a part of their family too. The two of them were the only friends she had, all she needed. But what if that was just something she told herself to make herself feel better? What if it was her way of coping with loneliness? Meloni realized that she was lonely. She had skills, she had a reputation that made people shudder, she had a family, but she didn't have a true companion. Maybe it was stupid to think of the doctor as a companion. He was untrustworthy, after all. After she saw what he did to those bandits earlier that day, she knew for a fact that he wasn't only a medic, if he was a medic at all.

He treated his cuts and wounds professionally and even wrapped his knuckles. That didn't say anything, though. Meloni could do the same thing. It was something one learned when living in a world where you had to fight for survival.

"When I was a kid," he said out of the blue, not even moving his head to look at her. He was speaking as if he was telling himself a story. "My mother used to tell me that there were angels up there, looking down at us. I never understood why they would just look down and do nothing to make the world a better place. I used to climb to the very top of containers and talk to them. I used to ask them to please come down and bring me a piece of the moon, so I can wear it around my neck. I thought the moon was a giant, glowing orb that could act as a torch in the darkness. I've always hated the dark."

"I asked them if they could bring an army with them so they could defeat the bad guys and rebuild the world. Surely they saw what was going on if they were looking down at us all the time. As the years progressed, I developed a deep hatred for these angels. I came to the conclusion that they liked to see the world suffer. I thought they were sadists, reveling in the torment that has befallen the earth. I was only twelve when she passed away. The plague had wiped out most of the adults in my camp. The only way I managed to cope was clinging onto the one thing she told me: 'the dead become angels too.' I was convinced that she would rally the other angels and gather the troops to swoop down from the heavens to save us. That day never came." Meloni's heart felt as if it was being crushed. She watched his profile that was illuminated by the moon. His strong brow was relaxed. It wasn't a painful memory for him, she realized. He was too casual, and his face was too relaxed. In the two days she's known him, she began picking up on his habits. He furrowed his brow when he was serious and massaged his hands when he was thinking. He smiled to hide a wealth of pain, and she began to realize that he wasn't as tough as he wanted everyone to believe he was.

In that moment, she could see that little blond boy on the roof, watching the stars. She could see it as clearly as if it was real.

"I never knew my father, so when my mother died, I was left on the streets, and I had to learn how to fight for survival. The other orphans often stole from me when I wasn't in my alley, so I planted traps and plotted ambushes to catch them. I had to survive long enough for my mother to come back, you know? I couldn't have them steal my things. But one day, a trap of mine backfired, and I was badly burned. My leg was one giant blister, and I was certain I was going to die with a fever. I have never been in that much pain my entire life. And then one day, while I was stretched out on my bedroll next to a trash can behind a bar, a medic found me. He took me back to his room in an inn where he treated the burns. I was in and out of a fevered sleep the entire time, but I remember him telling me a story about the stars too. He said that they were only balls of gas that people often worshipped and clung to for hope. He told me that if some people could cling to balls of gas for hope, I had to cling to life for my own hope. His story with the balls of gas made much more sense than the angels, and I accepted that my mother was wrong all along."

"Is that why you became a medic?" Meloni's voice was soft, and she thought she might have to repeat herself because he took a while to answer.

"I guess. Later I learned that he was from the capital, sent all around the wasteland to help the people who were attacked by mercenaries or Nighters or whatever. He had to leave soon after I recovered and I never saw him again. When I moved to the capital, I half-hoped that I would run into him again. I never even knew his name. All I knew was that I had a stranger to thank for my life. I wanted to be that hope for other people too." Meloni smiled. It was a good story. A story that felt as if she took a trip into the past and saw him. She had a feeling that he didn't share these things often. He was like her. It was hard to let people in. He was making an effort. They were going to be on the road for a good couple of days more. She figured it was her turn to make an effort.

"About a year ago, I decided that I wanted to run away and find my own home in the wasteland." Bryce turned his head toward her slightly to see her face as she was telling the story. She gave him a sideways smile. "I was sick of being the Ghost. I didn't want to do odd jobs anymore, and I knew that I had the skills to be more. I just had to find the right place to settle. The bunker is home, yes, but I felt like I had to build my own, you know? I was 23 at the time, and I was sick of staying with my brother. We had some stupid fight about a job, and I took off. I didn't take food, water, or a sleeping bag. I didn't even think that far. All I knew was that I had to get away."

"I never traveled for longer than a day at that point and didn't know what horrors the nights in the wastelands held. I've always heard rumors, and I heard the Nighters at night, but never really encountered them. I thought that I was very smart, and if I kept moving, they wouldn't find me."

"You were in the wasteland alone at night? Without anything?" Bryce let out a whistle and shook his head.

Meloni shrugged, "Pretty much. The first night I ran into trouble. A horde of Nighters had tracked me for miles and then finally surrounded me. I had nowhere to go. I tried to fight them, but there were so many of them." Meloni shivered involuntarily. "They captured me and took me back to their lair. I knew that they were going to present me to their leader before eating me. I just knew it."

"You must have been terrified."

"I was," she admitted. "I have never experienced that level of fear ever again. They were creatures like in the myths. Their teeth were sharp, and their eyes were nearly swollen shut. I could see their malformed spines through their skin. They roughed me up pretty bad before my rescue came. Michael and Carter arrived in a reinforced truck that Carter 'borrowed' from the guard. They risked their lives to save me from the most horrific beings I have ever seen." As if on cue, a particularly loud growl echoed through the empty wasteland, and it sent shivers down her spine. She was grateful for the climb they had made when they saw the high structure that afternoon. The higher up they were, the safer.

"How did they find you?"

Meloni chuckled and shook her head. "My bastard brother sewed a tracker into the back of my shirt while I was sleeping a couple of weeks prior. They tracked me to the cave."

"I've never encountered a Nighter," was all Bryce said.

"Even hearing them, I can feel the scars they left on my body pulse. Some of them even bit me." She lifted her shirt up slightly to expose the bite mark on her lower abdomen even though it was nearly impossible to see in the lighting. Meloni traced the outline. "It's why I need to find Michael, no matter what. He took on an entire horde of Nighters for me. What sort of a sister will I be if I don't take on the wasteland for him?"

"He didn't do it to have you in his debt, Meloni. You know that, right?" She never thought about it like that. Was she so determined to save him to return the favor? No, she didn't think so.

"I know. He did it because we are family, and that's what family does. We save each other, no matter what the situation might be. I will get him back, even if I have to take on the Scorpion myself."

She could see a faint smile on Bryce's face. "The poor bastard won't know what hit him."

NINE

A Familiar Face

IT WAS THE FOURTH DAY OF THEIR JOURNEY. MELONI WAS growing increasingly agitated and snippy. Bryce had told her that they would be traveling for a long time, but somehow, she had hoped it wouldn't take this long.

They weren't making nearly as much progress as they wanted to as they had to look for shelter and make detours for it. They were dead without shelter, and she knew that it was the truth. Still, it didn't increase her sour mood. What was she thinking? What the hell was she thinking? This wasn't worth the money Bryce promised, and she had to remind herself repeatedly of the reason she was really doing this. Michael needed her, and although she wished Bryce was wrong, she knew that he wasn't. The Barracks was the best place to get information on the notorious Smuggler. It was more hope than she had in weeks. She had to hold on to it.

"Your mind is working overtime," Bryce commented, and she found him looking at her from above. He held out a hand to pull her up the steep dune. How had he gotten up there? She took his hand.

"We need supplies, doc," she said as his large hand clamped around hers. They fit perfectly together. She looked at it for a moment before she was lifted from the ground and sat down beside him. One hand, he had used one hand.

"Look at where we're at, Ghostie," he said with a grin, and Meloni had to suppress a surprised giggle. They were at an oasis much larger than the one they met at.

The dam was as blue as the sky above. The sun bounced off it as if it was a jumping castle. She had never seen so much green in her entire life. It was beautiful, and her breath was taken away. She couldn't help but run toward it. She was drawn to it, not only by her parched throat but by the idea of swimming in that dam. The water probably wasn't as cool as she would have liked it to be, but there was a good chance that it would soothe her sore muscles and cool her down a bit.

It was hard to run in the sand, but she had a newfound strength in her legs that she hadn't had a day ago. From behind her, she heard Bryce laughing. The only sound that made her believe that he was following her was the rustle of his pack on his back.

When she reached the greenery, she stopped to look at the leaves, her swim forgotten for now. Was this what the world was like before the Great War? She heard stories, but she could never imagine it, never paint the picture. Now though; now she could. She could see the earth in this natural, green state. She could imagine the broken down building they've been sleeping in the past couple of nights restored and surrounded by trees, shrubs, and patches of grass.

Bryce led her past the trees and she reluctantly followed, picking a leaf and holding it in her hand as they went. She didn't take her eyes off it. Meloni never knew anything could be so beautiful. She wanted to stay here forever. She never wanted to leave.

Her eyes were drawn away from the leaf as they approached the clear, blue water. Bryce was the first to kneel down and take a large sip of the water. He moaned as it licked his throat. Without thinking, Meloni dropped her pack and stripped off her clothes. Leaving only her underwear on which consisted of boy shorts and a sport's bra. She ran into the water with a child's enthusiasm, the water surprisingly cool the deeper she got. The top layer was hot. But the water around her feet, legs, and hips was cool. She moaned at the sensation and splash in the water told her that Bryce had the same idea. He dove under the surface of the water, and the water was so clear, she could watch him swim past her and re-emerge. He grinned at her, droplets of water gathering on his eyelashes and his chest glistening from wetness. It was probably one of the most glorious sights she has ever seen. Second only to the view of the oasis from the top of that dune.

Bryce took her hand and led her deeper into the water. Meloni didn't know how deep it was, and she didn't trust herself to be a skilled enough swimmer to go deeper than where her feet could touch the ground below. He led her only deep enough for the water to reach her neck, and he had to bend his knees to get on the same eye-level as her.

They looked at each other then. They didn't say a single word, but Meloni found that there was nothing she really wanted to say. She just wanted that moment to last. In that moment, Meloni was not the Ghost. She wasn't looking for her brother, dedicating every moment of every day to rescuing him. In that moment, she shooed away the trust issues and accepted that she was just a girl, taking a swim with a handsome man. She wanted to give in to him. Over the few days they've been traveling, he hasn't forced himself on her but has made it clear that he wanted her. Meloni would lie if she said she hadn't considered it multiple times, but now, at this moment, was the first time she could imagine it.

Their attention was snapped to roaring engines and battle cries. It had to be mercenaries. Bandits didn't use vehicles. Their other enemies were either mute, deformed, or dim. It wasn't the guards either, no; they didn't have the barbaric ways of shouting their battle cries before even spying on the enemy.

Bryce let out a string of curses that would make a sailor cringe and dove back under the water, their moment lost.

Meloni was dumbstruck for a moment before slowly wading her way out of the water. Bryce already held multiple weapons in his hands. Her weapons. She found that she didn't mind it. She should have given him Michael's extra weapons when they first started the journey. He still had a chance with his bare hands against the bandits, but she wasn't so sure about the mercenaries. They had guns and training, something the bandits did not. They didn't bother dressing for the occasion of an ambush. Instead, they grabbed everything they could, including the rifle she had stuffed in her bag that she took from the other mercenary, and waited. The trees gave them enough shade to protect them from the sun, and there was no time for them to get dressed. They had to choose between being dressed and being prepared. Bryce's boxer shorts clung to his thighs, and she was under no illusion that he wasn't angry that he was caught in this state. They were stupid and let their guard down, and it might just cost them their life.

They stood back to back, not exchanging a single word. It was as if they could read each other's minds. They had to have each other's backs if they wanted to survive.

There was a rustle in the trees next to them. Before Meloni could react, Bryce was in front of her, a hunting blade in each hand as he sliced down the merc. He crumbled into a heap on the ground before him before an entire group circled them.

She pressed her back against Bryce's, their bare skin touching for the first time and probably the last. Her heart raced, and her ears rang.

No, they were not going to die like this. Not before she found Michael, not before she had her moment with Bryce, and definitely not before she's been with a man for the first time.

She eyed the mercenaries. They were ready to jump, to attack at any moment, and then her eyes fell on one in particular. The owner of the rifle she was holding. The mercenary she spared when she could have killed him.

Without the mask, he probably didn't recognize her. They were merely two lovebirds that they happened to catch.

"We are from the Barracks," the man spoke with more authority than she remembered him having. "You will come with us as our prisoners, or you will die."

Bryce snorted. "It's funny that you think ten men are enough to beat my partner and me."

Meloni caught on, and she grinned. "You know," she purred in the same, raspy tone she used on the man the first time they met. "I haven't had the chance to test out your rifle yet. Should I shoot you first, or your companions?"

Recognition settled on his face, and he took a step back. Then, as if remembering, he outnumbered them, smiled at her. "The Ghost is revealed."

Meloni shrugged, "If I knew you were coming, I

would've at least put my mask on. But now that you've seen my face, I guess my only option is to kill you."

Her words sparked something in the men surrounding them, and they attacked. The gunshot was probably audible for miles, but she didn't care. The man in front of her had a hole in his head, and he fell to the ground. Behind her, she could tell that Bryce was fighting his own way through the men and grunts and groans filled the air that surrounded the oasis. She felt guilty for contaminating it, somehow.

Another man was upon her, and she didn't have time to aim the rifle. Instead, she used the back end of it to bash the man's face in. His nose crunched, and he stumbled back. Three men grabbed her from her side, and the rifle fell to the ground. Their grip was like iron, and she let out a guttural wail. Shit, shit, shit!

She had to think, had to make a plan. She looked at Bryce, whose face blanched when he fought off his last attacker and saw Meloni being dragged back to the car. Meloni swore at the attackers, threatening them with painful and merciless deaths. They didn't even falter, and in that moment, she knew that her hours were numbered. They'd take her back to the Barracks who had no doubt recruited the encampment she raided a few days ago to their army. They had fortresses all over the wasteland, and their prisoners of battle were the ones who were forced to build them. She didn't want to think about what their plans were with her. She was the Ghost. Perhaps, they'd shoot her in the head just to make a point.

She was ripped from the men's arms, and she yelped as she was tossed aside. Away from the hell that was about to break loose. She watched as Bryce aimed the rifle at the men and shot one after the other with deadly precision. The owner of the rifle was already in the driver's seat when the last of his companions fell. All they could do was watch as he sped away, leaving nine corpses and two living targets behind.

Meloni has never been so embarrassed in all her life. She was a better fighter than this. She had taken on more men single-handedly. Was this the level of skill the Barracks guards had? Was it enough to out-skill the mighty Ghost?

"Where did you learn to fight like that?" Meloni asked as she approached him. He turned to her, his brows creased.

He handed her the rifle as he turned back toward the oasis and their things. His shoulders were already turning red from the exposure to the sun. She had no doubt she looked like a tomato herself. "I lied when I said I was a medic for the capital," was all he said. It was all he had to say.

"You are a medic for the Barracks…" Meloni finished his sentence for him. He nodded gravely.

"Why aren't they looking for you?"

He started walking, and she had to jog to keep up. "They are. But they are looking for a lone traveler, not two."

"If you are running from the Barracks, why are we heading there?" So many things finally made sense, but so many mysteries presented themselves in their place.

"Because, Meloni," he snapped as he turned to her, pointing at the gash on his neck. "They are the ones responsible for this."

THEY DIDN'T TALK MUCH after the attack. They filled their water bottles and got dressed, shared a small portion of dried meat as it was nearly finished and headed North again. The trail which the car left in the sand was already being blown away by the wind, and Meloni found her mind wandering to dark places.

She saw Bryce tied to a chair while they brutalized him. There were wounds in his eyes that she has never noticed before, but once she's seen them, she couldn't un-see it.

That night, they found an old tool shed that made her bunker look like a mansion. It was too small for their sleeping bags to be apart, so they had to push them next to each other, almost overlapping. They sat in silence for a good hour or two after the sun had set. The shed had no roof, but at least they were sheltered from the sides. If a Nighter had the brains to climb the shed, they were screwed.

"You don't have to come with me if you don't want to," Bryce finally said, his head resting against the wall. "The mission isn't exactly what I told you it was."

"I knew that there was something more to this journey," Meloni shrugged, looking at him. She wished they had a light so she could see more than just the outline of his face. Her heart felt like it was being crushed. For all the arrogance and cocky smiles, this man was deeply damaged. Just like she was. He had her back in the fight, went after her, and has saved her life twice now. It was time for her to let go of the doubt and trust him. If he didn't let her die by now, he wasn't going to any time soon. He would stay true to his word and find out what he could about her brother, and he would pay her for the journey as well. This meant food and perhaps some new shoes. Those were the thoughts that went through her head when he mentioned money at the very beginning, but now she found herself not caring as much. She wanted to be on this journey with him. Despite the danger, she hasn't enjoyed herself this much in ages. It was worth it. "I'm not going home until we're done."

"Weren't you the one who wanted to leave a few days ago?" he nudged Meloni with his shoulder.

"That was before I knew you actually had some depth."

Bryce roared with laughter, and the sound made her stomach turn.

"I'm glad I found you that day."

"So I could be your disguise?" Meloni raised an eyebrow even though she knew he couldn't fully see it.

"You're not my disguise, Meloni. At first, maybe. But not anymore."

Her throat tightened and she swallowed. "And what am I now?"

"Now, you are my partner."

Then, without thinking about the consequences of their mission or the danger that surrounds them, Meloni swallowed her doubt and settled herself on Bryce's nap.

He didn't wait for her to second-guess her decision. He kissed her.

He kissed her like she had always imagined being kissed. It was hungry and passionate, yet tender in a way that made her feel as fragile as the kiss was. Meloni draped her arms over his shoulders, and he pulled her closer by the small of her back. She was so small compared to him, and yet they fit together so perfectly. Just like their hands did. His other hand was on the back of her head, pulling on her hair in a way that made her gasp and moan simultaneously.

She never wanted to forget that feeling. She never wanted to forget the passion that danced between them in such a sweet tango. This was it for her. She didn't think it was going to get any better.

But then he rolled her over, so he was hovering above her. He bit her lip and smiled when she squealed. His hips were between her legs, and he gently held her hands above her head in a firm grip. She thought the kiss was the best part, but that was before the doctor made sweet love to the Ghost.

TEN

Surprise!

MELONI AWOKE TO THE SUN PEERING IN THROUGH THE open roof. What a nosy thing it was. Couldn't it leave them alone for a single day?

She felt a heavy arm draped over her waist, clinging to her like the owner of that arm's life depended on it. That arm was connected to a bare torso that pressed against her bare back. She could feel his breath on her hair. It wasn't as deep as someone deep in slumber, but instead it was the calm breathing of a person who was perfectly content. The second clue was that he wasn't snoring. As soon as that man closed his eyes, the grizzly showed up.

"Good morning," he purred in her ear. Goosebumps ran down her body and her toes curled. His voice was rough and raspy, still a little bit sleepy.

She turned around in his arms to face him, grinning up at his wild hair. He was gorgeous. He was strikingly gorgeous. She kissed his lips gently.

"Does your body hurt as much as mine?" He raised an eyebrow at her question with a slight smirk plastered on his face. She smacked his chest. "No, you pervert. Not like that. I can't wait to get home and sleep on a mattress again."

"Then let's head home," he said after a moment of silence. Meloni frowned.

"What happened to getting your revenge?"

"That was before I got something else."

She contemplated it for a moment, and then shook her head. "No, we see this through. We're nearly there, aren't we? I need information. You need to do whatever it takes to settle that rage you have inside of you. If revenge is what it takes, then revenge is what you'll get."

"You can't come with me."

"Like hell," she protested. "I can hold my own and you know it."

"Yes, like you did with the mercs that dragged you away?"

"I wasn't prepared. Now I will be. If they don't know that I'm coming, I can pick them off one by one without losing a single bullet."

The doctor reached over and took her dog tags in his hand. "What if he isn't there?"

"What if he is? What if the Scorpion has him?"

"The Scorpion doesn't have him."

"How do you know? He's the head of the Barracks, isn't he?"

"That is merely a rumor. He isn't the man you think he is. Dangerous, yes, but not that evil. He would never take slaves and burn down camps."

"You know who he is, don't you?"

Bryce nodded. "Known him most of my life. Trust me when I tell you that you do not have to worry about the Scorpion. In fact, I'm pretty sure he is on our side."

"Anything else you wish to share with me? A secret family, perhaps?"

Bryce laughed. "I didn't lie when I said I have no family." He took a deep breath. "Okay, gorgeous. If we are going to do this, we'll need to get a move on. We're losing daylight and we need to go if we want to make it to the next shelter before nightfall. It's close to the Barracks. We can make it there tonight and scout a little tomorrow, perhaps get some food. I'm already starving. There's only one bun left."

Meloni pulled a face. The bread was stale and started to get moldy. She wanted to avoid eating it for as long as possible.

Deciding on the best route, the companions gathered their clothes and rolled up their sleeping bags. Meloni's heart raced. They were really going to do it. She tried to be tough, tried to harness the Ghost's fearlessness, but she couldn't. She had more than one man in her life to lose now. There was more at stake.

But when they stepped outside, all of their plans fell apart when a dozen armed men surrounded the shed. Bryce instinctively pulled her behind him to protect her. Panic overtook her body and she couldn't move, couldn't say a single thing.

Her old acquaintance emerged from the guards, and he held a smirk that would haunt her dreams. She should have killed him in that studio. It was proving to be the biggest mistake of her life.

"I was ordered to kill you both," he drawled, then pointed to the orange bandana covering Bryce's face. "But that bandana means that you are useful. So you will be coming with us."

The circle around them shrunk and Meloni felt claustrophobic. She was the Ghost. She was the Ghost. She was the Ghost.

"Kill the bitch."

"Wait!" Bryce said, pulling the bandana from his face. "You've seen me fight. I can take down all of you without my lady having to lift a finger." The men looked at each other. "But I will come without a fight if you let the girl go."

Every man turned to look at their leader, who shrugged and nodded. "He has a point. Take him and the supplies. She won't get far without them."

"Bryce," Meloni croaked as he took a step toward the men, his hands in the air.

"Don't come after me," he said. "Go home."

She wanted to open her mouth to protest, but her pack was ripped from her back by strong hands and she was shoved to the sand. How was she going to survive long enough to get home? How was she going to live with herself knowing that yet another man has sacrificed himself to keep her safe? She couldn't. She wouldn't. She got to her feet and lunged toward the man who took her pack. She was reckless and the doctor shouted her name, but she didn't listen. She paid dearly for her stupidity.

The merc was faster than she was, and used her own blade to stab her in the side.

"Meloni!" Bryce shouted, but the men were on him before he could get to her. They manacled his hands and feet before he could fight them.

The leader roared with laughter as he walked toward her. She was faintly aware of the pain in her stomach. When had she fallen to the ground? Where was Bryce? The familiar face crouched over her and grinned. "You never should have made me look like a fool," he said, before snapping the chain around her neck. He held the dog tags in his hand, examining them. "I'll take those. It's not as if you'll be needing them anymore."

ELEVEN

Fever

MELONI KNEW THAT SHE WAS GOING TO DIE. SHE COULD feel it in her bones.

After the mercenaries sped away and she watched her only hope disappear in the distance, she managed to crawl into the shed and kicked the door closed.

She tried to remember everything she knew about medicine, about treating wounds and avoiding infections. She didn't have anything she needed to keep the wound from getting septic. Her adrenaline was wearing off quickly. The shed was mostly bare and the tools that still hung on the walls were corroded and useless. This was the end. This was where she left the earth, never to be seen or heard from again.

Meloni tried to put as much pressure on the wound as she could, even managed to shrug off her cloak and wrap it haphazardly around her stomach. There was no way that the injury wasn't going to get infected. There was too much dirt and her blade... her blade had killed multiple men and she never bothered to clean it aside from wiping it on her pants. She was either going to die from the infection, or from bleeding out. She figured she had a better chance at survival if she stopped at least one of those.

Her world exploded in pain whenever she moved and she settled into a corner with the most shade.

Time was a merciless beast that showed no mercy to mankind. It didn't slow when the moments were good, and it didn't go by faster when there was pain, heartache, or death. Instead, it continued at its own pace, not caring about the effects it had on the human mind.

There were several hours of daylight left. It was only morning after all and the sun wasn't close to reaching its highest point. Meloni had nothing but time until death finally claimed her. Time to think about the horrible things that happened to her, about the horrible things awaiting the doctor. She had nothing but time to think about her brother, about Carter, who would forever believe she was still mad at him about their exchange the other night about Bryce, who she had just found something with. She wasn't sure what that something was yet, but she knew that it was something good, something great.

She barely felt the tears run down her face as she wept.

"I failed them," she whispered to herself. "I failed them, I failed them, I failed them. I failed them all."

Meloni allowed herself to fall into a well of self-pity. There was nothing else to do anyway.

She had lost her companion, the man she may or may not have grown a fondness of. She had lost her brother and she failed to get him back. Two men have sacrificed themselves for her, and for what? So she could die in a filthy shed because she couldn't think further than her own rage? So she could throw away her name, her future?

Her sobs came more rapidly now. She wiped her nose angrily.

While she was throwing this pity party, she might as

well celebrate the fact that she had lost all her money and her brother's tags as well. She wasn't going to get new shoes, and she was going to die with an empty stomach. It growled on cue.

She had lost everything in a matter of minutes.

That morning she was still alive with a will to live. She wanted to live. She had an image of a future for the first time in a very, very long time, and it was stripped away from her. She had just learned the pleasures of being a woman with a man. She had just learned to appreciate a man's body for more than brute strength and protection. How cruel was the world to give her a taste of it only to strip it away before she could take a bite to fully appreciate it. It let her lick it, smell it, then yanked it away like a bully when she wanted to bite down on it. Life was cruel, this wasteland was cruel. Everything was against her and her happiness.

Perhaps this was for the greater good. Maybe, just maybe it was better to leave this world behind, to leave it all behind for a better world.

She thought about Bryce's mother's idea about the stars. She decided that she wanted to believe in that. She wanted to be a part of the stars. She wanted to believe that there was something better beyond this wretched world.

Meloni closed her eyes and thought about that life. It wasn't long until she fell into unconsciousness. Meloni dreamed about floating above the world with the people that have lived in the past. Perhaps she'd find her happy ending in death.

MELONI WAS twelve again and her hunting knife was still a little too big for her small hands. She's always been smaller than her age suggested.

Michael was standing in front of her in a fighting stance. He looked ready to attack, his navy blue eyes dancing with entertainment. He enjoyed training her as much as she enjoyed being trained. She loved getting better at things. Meloni always had one goal and one goal only; she wanted to be a better fighter than Michael ever was. She wanted to prove herself to him.

Michael lunged at her. Meloni skillfully sidestepped his attack, kicking out a leg to trip him.

Michael was the one who taught her that trick and avoided it with grace, grinning like a maniac as he turned to look at her.

"You're getting good, MelBell," he praised as they resumed their fighting stances. This time it was Meloni's time to attack and she was on the ground faster than she could think to dodge his leg. She groaned when she tasted dirt, her stomach where he had kicked her sensitive to the touch. "But not good enough, just yet."

"I'm never going to get good enough," she huffed, turning on her back to look at the sky.

Michael lied down next to her, poking her in the ribs. "Of course you are. You're already much faster than me. All you need is a little practice."

"All we do is practice," Meloni crossed her arms.

"Just hang in there," his words rang in her head. "Just hang in there, MelBell."

"YOU'VE FAILED everyone who ever cared about you," her own voice told her. It was her twelve-year-old self standing in front of her broken body that was covered in sweat and heaving. "No wonder you're all alone. You just let everyone down."

"That's not true," her adult self croaked. "I tried. I tried my best."

"That wasn't good enough, was it? You are a failure. No wonder your mother didn't want you. Your father left before you were even born. He was smart. He knew what a disappointment you'd become."

"Shut up," she hissed at the child.

"A complete and utter failure. A disgrace to humanity. The world will be a better place without you. All you do is kill and get the people around you killed. The doctor was taken because of you. He gave up his life for you. What an idiot. Couldn't he see that you weren't worth it?" The little girl's voice was sinister. Her head twitched. She repeated her sing-song words. "A complete and utter failure. A disgrace to humanity. The world will be a better place without you. All you do is kill and get the people around you killed. The doctor was taken because of you. He gave up his life for you. What an idiot. Couldn't he see that you weren't worth it? A complete and utter failure. A disgrace to humanity. The world will be a better place without you. All you do is kill and get the people around you killed. The doctor was taken because of you. He gave up his life for you. What an idiot. Couldn't he see that you weren't worth it?"

Meloni covered her ears, but the little girl's voice echoed in her head. "A complete and utter failure. A disgrace to humanity. The world will be a better place without you. All you do is kill and get the people around you killed. The doctor was taken because of you. He gave up his life for you. What an idiot. Couldn't he see that you weren't worth it?"

It repeated over and over again.

Her brother's voice was the last thing she heard. "Just hang in there, MelBell."

MELONI WAS at the oasis with the doctor again. They were in the pool, kissing each other like lovers from a bad romance novel. She could feel his touch on her skin, almost as if it were real. The kiss felt like it had that previous night. Her hands were in his luscious locks, pulling and pressing him closer to her. She knew she was dying, but he didn't. He didn't seem to notice the blood in the water surrounding them. He didn't see the wound in her side or the droplets of sweat on her brow. He kissed her despite the dirt and grime. Despite the red color of the blood on her hands that was staining his hair.

She wanted to tell him. To ask him for help. He was a doctor. He could save her, couldn't he? Why couldn't she speak? She couldn't move her mouth away from the kiss.

Only when they were joined by a dozen men and women did he pull away from her. His words dripped like poison from his lips as he let go of her waist. She had no strength to keep herself upright, so she floated in an animated way in the pool. "A complete and utter failure. A disgrace to humanity. The world will be a better place without you. All you do is kill and get the people around you killed. I was taken because of you. I gave up my life for you. What an idiot. Couldn't I see that you weren't worth it? Why did I think that being with you was a good idea? You are death incarnate."

Again and again, he chanted it. He was joined by the people around them. They closed in on them, wading their way through the bloody water before they reached her. She couldn't stop them as they pushed her beneath the surface. She couldn't fight off their hands. She couldn't hear their chanting anymore. Instead, it was replaced with another voice. A voice that nursed her wounds instead of making them worse.

It was the doctor's voice this time.

"Just hang in there, Ghostie."

MELONI WAS BACK in the shed. This time she wasn't the one on the floor, but the one looking down at her limp body. Her brother stood on her left, Bryce, on her right.

They looked at the body for a good minute, none of them saying a thing. Was this real? Did they see her? Was she a ghost that was looking down at her dead body? Were they all ghosts? Meloni spoke, called out their names, but they didn't respond. She really was a ghost.

She looked down at her hands. They were covered in black gloves. She was wearing her Ghost uniform.

Meloni was dead.

"No, no, no," she said, trying to rip the mask from her face. It was stuck in place. "I'm not dead. I'm not dead yet. I have things to live for, I have dreams. I'm not dead, I'm not dead!"

Suddenly the scene changed, and she was only one with her limp body. She no longer wore her black clothes.

Kneeling next to the body, she took her own hand in hers. The hand was hot. She wasn't dead, just unconscious. She had a bad fever, but she wasn't dead, not yet.

She lowered her head to the ear of the body and whispered the thing that she needed to hear. "You need to live, Meloni. Not survive; live." She swallowed a lump in her throat. "Just hang in there, Meloni."

TWELVE

Waking Up To a Confession

Meloni drifted in and out of consciousness. She felt as if she was floating on the surface of water. The waves lulling her in and out of sleep. It was a strange sensation and she wasn't sure what to make of it. She heard occasional talking, her brother, maybe, but that could have just been the fever. Of course, it was just the fever. There was no one around to talk to her. But the voice kept telling her to hold on, that he was going to save her. The voice never stopped, and she never stopped listening to it either. For that voice, whoever the owner was, hadn't let go of her just yet.

At one point, that voice was as clear as day. "I'm going to save you," he said. "Just hold on."

She felt something being pressed into her hand. Something cool and hard. She knew the feeling of those dog tags. She knew it like she knew her own body. It was a part of her. She clung to those tags for dear life, praying that they were real, that the voice was real.

But she knew she was hallucinating. She knew that she was clinging to false hope. She was dying alone. With her eyes still closed, Meloni realized that she was not dead and that, although the pain in her side was still aching, she didn't feel as weak anymore.

She dared to open her eyes.

She wasn't in the shed anymore. Instead, she was in a closed room, on a bed with a roof over her head. In a drugged state, she looked to her side and found a particular blond asleep on the floor, one pack tucked under his head and the other close by. He was sleeping on hers... Was it to protect her things or to smell her on the bag? She didn't know which it was, but she felt herself smiling at both thoughts. She never thought she'd be so happy to hear his snoring. It was comforting to listen to it. It was like music to her ears.

Meloni didn't sit up, didn't trust herself not to tear the wound open again, which he had obviously patched up judging by the bloody rag in his hand. The fever had taken a toll on her body, she could feel it. Her mind was still a bit groggy, too, but all in all, she felt good.

She felt good to be alive. She knew she was alive because of the dread in her stomach and the pain in her side. Dead people weren't supposed to feel. That was how she distinguished between being asleep and conscious too. In the dreams, she didn't feel the pain. It was in those horrible moments that she was alone in the shed, hand still pressed as tightly as she possibly could over the wound that was the most painful. Both physically and mentally. When she was conscious, she didn't see them anymore. Even if they said horrible things to her in her dreams, at least they were there. At least they were with her. She wasn't alone.

But now she was awake, and she wasn't alone either.

She faintly remembered the dog tags being pressed into her palms. When she brought her hand up, she realized that they were real. She didn't dream it. Her brother was there, giving her the tags, telling her to hold on. With a smile on her face, Meloni fell back into a deep sleep. This time without terrible dreams, without any dreams at all, actually. She just slept and slept and slept.

MELONI WOKE up as the sun was rising, and her mind wasn't dense with fog anymore. She was able to think clearly. She could hear her own thoughts again, she could recall memories.

She looked over to where she remembered seeing the doctor. He was still sleeping, the rag in his hand and a gun in the other. Her brother's pistol that she had buried at the bottom of her pack before they left the hole.

As if sensing that someone was watching him, Bryce opened his eyes and met hers. His green eyes danced when he saw her. The biggest smile she had ever seen on him split his face. Meloni couldn't help but mirror the smile. It made her cheeks hurt, but she didn't care. She was alive, and he was to thank for it yet again. It was the third time now.

"Honestly," he drawled as he pushed himself up with one arm, waving the gun around like a maniac. "I'm not going to save your ass again."

Meloni chuckled and realized that her side didn't hurt nearly as much as it was supposed to. "I didn't ask you to save me this time."

"Oh, I believe you did," he said. "Well, not in as many words, but you did repeatedly tell yourself to hold on. I figured it was your cry for help."

Meloni sat up. She noticed she wore a clean t-shirt and pants. She frowned. "Um, can you please explain to me what happened and how we got here? Actually, where are we anyway?"

Bryce pushed himself up against the wall, the sun peeking in through the window, caressing his face. He sighed. "I have a confession to make. And I need you to listen until the very end before you decide to throw me out the window."

"I can't make any promises, but I will try to keep quiet. What's going on?"

"My name is Bryce Harrow, also known as the Scorpion." There was a short intake of breath. Meloni realized that it was hers. She frowned but nodded for him to continue. If he were finally coming clean, Meloni would let him. She owed him that much for saving her life. "Everything I told you about my childhood was true. I grew up in a small camp, lost my mother, and was saved by a medic. The one thing I lied about was that the medic took me to the Barracks with him. He wasn't one of the capital's doctors. Instead, he was from the Barracks, sent to recruit orphans for the army.

They trained me, fed me, trained me some more. I learned everything I could from the medic who took me in. It made me valuable to the cause, they said. The more things I could do, the better I would be for the army.

I let them brainwash me into thinking that I was nothing but a weapon. I raided camps and took slaves. I blew up entire towns and oversaw the construction of multiple fortresses across the wasteland. But one day, I met a slave woman. I have never seen anyone like her. I did my best to woo her. It worked, and nine months later, she gave birth to a beautiful baby boy. I named him Nicholas. I hid him from the Barracks. Nicholas and his mother. I was trying to get out, trying to hang up my rifle and move to a peaceful camp with my lovely lady and our son. I wanted to marry her," his voice croaked. "I even had a ring ready for the day we could leave. But somehow, one of my men found out about my hidden family after years of keeping them a secret. Nicholas was only four when the guards barged into my container and found them. They made me watch as they stripped Celise and whipped her. She screamed my name. I couldn't do anything. I was helpless, held down by seven guards.

Then they took my boy to the commander and-"

"Bryce," Meloni said with tears in her eyes, but he ignored her. He went on with a steady voice. She didn't know how he was able to tell this story.

"The commander put a gun to his head and blew his brains out. Just like that. He didn't give him a chance to train or join the army like the rest of the orphans they took in. He wanted to make a point. Anyone who disobeyed his orders got punished. He moved on to me next. They spent days on me, kept me shirtless in the sun, whipped me, beat me close to death, but stopped just before they sealed my fate. I begged them for death. I was heartbroken. Then one day, I decided that I was going to get out of that hellhole and take my sweet time with revenge. But my plans were interrupted when they took me out into the desert and slit my throat. They didn't bother watching me die. That was their first mistake."

"What was their second?"

Bryce smiled. "I'm still getting to that part." He straightened his back and sat taller. "I had enough medical training to keep myself from bleeding out. I didn't have the means to seal the wound properly, so the scar would heal less harsh, but I survived nonetheless. I think that in a way, I did die, though, and only a part of me survived. That part became the Scorpion. I vowed to make their life hell."

Things didn't make full sense to Meloni. "I thought you were the leader of the Barracks?"

Bryce laughed. "It was a rumor I started to piss the officials off. Their denials just made it more believable that I was pulling the strings and they didn't want anyone to know it."

"But why take on the Barracks now? You've been active as the Scorpion for over five years."

"I only recently found out that they were taking more slaves to their fortresses. I always knew about what they did and why they did it. Cheap labor and all, but then I found out that they had killed the medic that took me in because he let a traitor into the camp. How could he have known? He was the only person who ever loved me like a father loves a son, or at least that was what I thought a father's love should feel like. They tortured him for years until they finally had mercy on him and killed him."

"But they don't know that you are the Scorpion? They think that you are dead? Why did you have to take me along with you?"

The Scorpion sighed. "They thought I was dead, and they didn't know I'm the Scorpion. They know now. And as far as you are concerned," he gave her a lover's smile, "I have been infatuated with you before I even knew you. The woman that moved like a Ghost. The only person who had made a name for herself as big as the Scorpion. Then I saw you on that elevator shaft. I knew exactly who you were. I needed someone to distract me from my rage. I knew I couldn't do it alone, and you presented yourself to me on a silver platter."

Meloni didn't know what to make of it. He really was in the camp picking up supplies when he saw her by chance. He never wanted her to get him there; he wanted her help to take them down. He was the Scorpion who idolized her. Her head spun.

"Then things got out of hand between the two of us in the best possible way. I knew that I couldn't risk you the same way I risked Celise. But I underestimated your will to get your brother, and I understood the need you had to protect.

I fully intended to leave the Barracks be. Only get your brother out. Then those assholes attacked. I honestly thought you were dead. I fought the entire way there. I even threw two of them from the back of the truck until they sedated me and took me to the commander who recognized me from a mile away. His second mistake was throwing me in a cage with a certain raven-haired man that goes by the Smuggler."

Meloni sat up straighter. He saw Michael. Where was he? Was he here? Was he waiting to make a grand entrance?

"Don't look so excited. He's not here, but I know that he is alive and where exactly he is in the base. Turns out that little twerp lied to you about knowing where he was. Michael was in their prison the entire time, plotting his own escape. He was the one who caused the explosion we saw the day we met. He ran for dear life. The mercs chasing after him only to be caught by the Barracks' men. They joined forces and the mercs' prisoner became the Barracks' prisoner."

"I still don't know what to make of all this," Meloni admitted. "But that does sound like the sort of grand escape only my brother could pull off from a prison cell."

"I told your brother that you were with me. That you came for him. I told him about your wound. He helped me escape. He had planned to use the route himself, but he doesn't have the medical skills to save you. So, he gave me his escape plan instead. I don't even think they know I'm gone yet, but if they do, it's only a matter of time before they find us. I know you want to go back for your brother, and I will help you, but it's up to you how we do it. Personally, I want to kill every last one of them with my bare hands."

"No, we do this my way," Meloni said with newfound confidence. They had a lot to plan, and he still had a lot to tell her, but in that moment, she knew that he was telling her the complete truth for the first time since they met. She trusted him with her life. "We hit before they even know we're there. And then we take them all down from inside their own damned fortress. The prisoners will help, so they are our first priority."

"As you wish."

THIRTEEN

Scouting

ONLY LATER DID MELONI DISCOVER THAT BRYCE HAD carried her all the way to their next safe house close to the Barracks. He had to get her to a proper bed, he had claimed, and there was no space in the little shed to do the necessary procedure to stop the infection from spreading. So, the man patched her up as best he could, carried her for a good six hours, and then operated on her still when they reached the destination. She had to fight the urge to kiss him, to tell him that she didn't know what she'd do without him, but now wasn't the time. It wasn't the time for romance or feelings. They were too close to the Barracks to get distracted. Plus, they've surely found out by now that Bryce escaped. She wondered briefly what they were doing to her brother to find out how Bryce had gotten out. She inwardly cringed. Now was not the time for that. It was not the time to get distracted.

It was not the time.

She looked over at Bryce, who was trapped inside his own head for most of the morning. It seemed as if the closer they got to the Barracks fortress, the quieter he got.

They must have been very close because he hasn't said a single word, hasn't cracked a single smile in twenty minutes.

She didn't like it.

Not because she was worried about him; he was a grown man who could fight his own battles. He's proven that many times before. But because his muteness meant that Meloni was stuck in her own mind as well. Stuck in the mind that conjured a spirit image of her younger self to break herself down. Her mind that made the only people in her life real, and had them encourage her death. She knew that she could no longer trust her own mind. She had to battle herself to hold to life. She didn't know if that made her stronger or encouraged that dark part of her mind to do it again. Giving something attention usually encouraged it to do it again and again. She wasn't sure that she was going to survive that attack next time. Not if her darker mind had time to come up with better reasons why she should die. She knew that there were a lot of those lying around if only she looked hard enough.

Meloni shook those thoughts from her head. "No distractions," she told herself in a hushed voice. "No distractions."

Her mind didn't listen to her own advice. It was only when they reached the top of the dune that the voices in her head finally died down. Meloni gasped at the sight in front of her, her mouth suddenly dry.

They reached the fortress, and it was unlike anything she had ever seen.

It wasn't the sort of makeshift structures that one usually found around the wasteland, but instead, it was made of bricks like something from the old world. Meloni remembered looking at pictures of castles and fortresses as a child. Still, those pictures could never compare to the real thing.

There were massive watchtowers that surrounded the fortress, with draw bridge gates that were closed. They couldn't see inside the courtyard like she'd hoped.

At the very back was a large building that looked like a small castle. Meloni briefly imagined a man sitting on a throne, a crown on his head as he listened to the peasants complain. Was that how it was? Was the commander trying to build a kingdom for himself? Was that why they were building the other fortresses in the wasteland as well? They were slowly making their way to the capital. She knew that they didn't stand a chance if the Barracks attacked. They would suffer the same fate as so many of the smaller mercenary encampments have. How so many straggler camps have suffered? Meloni didn't care much about the people in the capital. They were all sheep anyway. But no person deserved to be forced into slavery the same way the commander was forcing the people of defeated camps to do his bidding. It had to end. It had to end before he caused more damage than he already has. If anyone stood a chance of defeating him, it was Meloni and Bryce. The Ghost and the Scorpion. They were skilled, and they were smart—things that she'd learned from Bryce's hour-long rants and information he told her that she had to memorize—the Barracks was not. They were reckless brutes and it might have worked for them until now, but they haven't dealt with her and Bryce's combined power yet.

She allowed herself to imagine their victory as they crept closer to the fortress, falling flat on their stomachs whenever Bryce thought someone was looking their way. Their cloaks were the exact shade as the sand and they blended in well. It was effective but time-consuming.

Meloni was tired by the time they reached the wall and she rest her back against it. She was gasping for air, and Bryce didn't even have the decency to look winded. She scowled when he was already busy making his way around the fortress and to the back, not giving her a chance to recover from the cruel military drill of an approach to the fortress.

Meloni followed him quietly. They both moved with feline grace, and there wasn't as much as a sound that escaped from their boots on the sand. They were invisible as well as silent. If they played this right, they would be in and out before anyone had the chance to notice. She only hoped that things went according to plan.

It took them nearly ten minutes to reach the back of the fortress, the walls spanning so vast that walking around it was a complete exercise on its own. At least the sun was a little more merciful that day. It wasn't the blistering heat that usually accompanied the time when the sun was at its highest. Still, it was a smoldering sort of heat. Subtle, but definitely there.

Bryce reached a grate that he pulled from its hinges with ease. The bolts have already been loosened. Was this how he had escaped in the first place? Was this how Michael planned on escaping? Probably, she didn't see any other way out from the fortress yet.

"Wait here," he said, looking over his shoulder to see if anyone was coming. There was no one there. "I'll talk to Michael to rally the prisoners and get a good count of the guards."

"What was the point of me coming with you if I just have to way out here?" she hissed in retort. She didn't appreciate being left out of plans, especially not plans that could cost her the life of her brother or her own.

"If I get caught, you have to know where to get in to

get me out," he said simply. "I am not dying in this place, so I am relying on you to get me out if things get ugly."

"Let me go in instead," Meloni said. "I'm smaller and will draw less attention. You are more skilled. I trust you with my life more than you should trust me with yours."

Bryce smiled for the first time in a good hour. He pulled her closer to him and pressed his lips to her fore-head. She melted into his embrace, wanted the moment to last forever. Meloni fought a shudder when he pulled away from her. The ghost of his kiss lingered on her forehead.

"I am going in. You are my hero if I get caught. Besides," he grinned as he got on all fours, preparing to crawl through the grate. "It's about time you saved my life for a change, don't you think?"

THEY WERE BACK at the safe house. Meloni tried to memorize the poorly drawn map Bryce had given her of the fortress. She asked him whether he got a child to draw it for him when he handed it over to her. He responded with a vulgar gesture and a mumble about unrecognized talent.

The building they were in wasn't a building as much as it was a room on stilts. Meloni imagined that it was once a hotel. Very similar to the hotel at the encampment her brother blew up. Instead of half of the hotel missing, everything was gone except for the one room and half of a bathroom on the floor below the room. They had to climb up the walls to reach it, where she often found herself wondering how Bryce had gotten her up there. How had he carried her, their packs, and the supplies he stole from the fortress up there? It must have been a few trips he had to make up and down the walls.

The map showed two entrances. The main gate which was lowered from the inside by a team of soldiers and the grate that led directly to the cell Michael was held in. It was luck; it was pure damn luck that the location of that grate was so conveniently placed.

The dungeons led to the courtyard of the fortress, which was basically the town center. There was glass of all kinds and shops that sold various goods. The dungeons were directly below the fortress. The direct entrance from the dungeon was sealed shut. This meant that they had to go through the courtyard first before they could get into the fortress.

It was a good thing they didn't plan on entering the fortress itself in the first place.

FOURTEEN

Busting Myths

THERE WAS A TALE THAT HER BROTHER USED TO TELL HER about the Scorpion. It was her favorite. Whenever she got somewhere where she can listen to new stories, she did in hopes that she would find one better than the one she was so in love with. She never did.

The story started in a wasteland. Much like any other story in the new world, and the Scorpion was feasting on a sand wolf he had killed with his bare hands. He didn't bother finding shelter for the night as the Nighters knew to avoid him at all costs. They didn't stand a chance against him, no matter the size of the horde they traveled in. Nothing stood a chance against a one-man army.

That night, as he was feasting, the group of sand wolves that he had killed the leader of for dinner, tracked him to his little fire. They were so outraged by the fact that they could smell the grilled flesh of their brother that they attacked the Scorpion. In typical Scorpion fashion, he didn't even get up from his seat on the sand. His legs still crossed, he used the stick that he was eating from as a weapon to defeat the wolves. It was over in less than a minute. When he was done, he was surrounded by a dead pack of sand wolves. He continued eating as if he wasn't even winded.

Now that Meloni knew the Scorpion on a personal level, she could see him telling his own story in a tavern where it was picked up by a gullible drunk and spread around. She could almost see the grin of satisfaction on his face when he heard the story being told all over the camp he was in. She didn't have to ask if he was the one to spread the story because she knew it was him. It was the sort of story only he could come up with.

They sat in the windowsill of the little room, looking at the stars the same way they had looked at it when he told her the story of his mother. It became a sort of tradition to them and Meloni couldn't say that she was against it at all. In fact, she found herself looking forward to the hour or two they spend staring at the stars. With the weather changing and nights growing cold, Bryce wrapped her in his arms the entire time. She reveled in the warmth of his touch. They didn't have to kiss, to make love for her to be happy. She was perfectly content sitting in his arms like that and watching his mind work.

"So," she started, a smile dancing on her face. "What was the inspiration behind the sand wolf story?"

In the moonlight, she could see him plaster a look of shock on his face, the fakeness almost animated. "What makes you think that I am the one who started it? Who says it never really happened?"

"Oh please," she giggled. "The story smells like something you cooked in that mind of yours."

Bryce sucked on a tooth before looking at her, his eyes dancing with mischief. "What version of the story did you hear?"

"That you were eating a sand wolf and his pack

attacked you. Apparently, you didn't even get up from where you were sitting and used the stick you used to grill the wolf to defeat his pack." Meloni raised an eyebrow, realizing just how ridiculous the story actually was. She wanted to kick herself for believing in it.

"Oh, it's taken an unexpected turn from the last time I told it," Bryce admitted. "The original story was far less flattering. In that one, I actually had to get my gun out to shoot them." Bryce put a finger to Meloni's forehead. "I don't know how anyone could believe I killed the wolves with a stick when their hides are like tires. Only a bullet to the head can kill them."

"Well," Meloni said as she rolled her eyes. "I know that much, at least."

"Did you believe that I did it with a stick?" There was humor in his voice, and she could tell that she was in for a night of teasing about this story.

"Before I met you, yes," she admitted.

"And now?"

"Now, dear mister Scorpion, I think that you are full of it."

"I've never denied that," he laughed.

"So, what was your inspiration, then?" Meloni prodded, and Bryce shook his head.

"I'll tell you, but then you'll answer my question." Meloni nodded, and he sighed. "When I was a kid, there was this shop in the camp where I used to hide from the other kids. They had magazines and comic books from floor to ceiling. I remember reading about an assassin so powerful; he could take out armies using only his mind. In one story, he was attacked by a horde of dragons. He chopped one of their heads off and used it as a flamethrower to burn the other dragons to death."

Meloni laughed. "So, you replaced the dragons with sand wolves?"

"Oh no," the Scorpion shook his head. "The original story had dragons, but for some reason, people didn't believe me when I told it."

"I wonder why." Meloni's words dripped with sarcasm.

Bryce shrugged. "I don't know who thought the sand wolves were more believable. They don't exist either."

"What? Of course they do."

"Do you believe in Santa and the tooth fairy too? They're about as real as the story."

Meloni furrowed her brows. "How do you know?"

"Ghostie, I have fought Nighters, mercs, and soldiers. I have spent weeks wandering the desert without shelter. If the sand wolves were real, I would have found them. I even spent a good month hunting for them. They are myths just like dragons, angels, and peace."

Meloni cringed at the morbid turn the conversation took. "What do you want me to answer?"

"I once heard a story about you, too, you know."

Meloni shook her head. "I've never spread stories about myself. Michael might have had something to do with it. Let's hear it."

"Well," Bryce said, clearing his throat. "If you haven't heard it before, then I guess I'll have to give you the full experience of a legendary, Scorpion storytelling."

"Can't be legendary if I've never heard of it."

"Do you want to hear the story or not?" he snapped, and Meloni threw her hands up in defeat. Only when he was sure that she wasn't going to interrupt him again did he start. "In a wasteland after the great war, there were things that adapted to the changes. Others that didn't. Some things died from the exposure, and others grew stronger, much stronger than humankind had the right to be.

"In that wasteland was a girl who bathed in darkness. The shadows were her source of power. It is said that the shadows pray to this girl, that they worship her as their queen for when she moves, no one sees her. When she strikes, no one hears her. She is only a shadow that fades into the darkness." Meloni got the chills as he spoke. Bryce seemed entranced by the story himself, and she didn't want to interrupt him. The story, even though wildly inaccurate, was entertaining. "This shadow girl went by the name of the Ghost. Not because she moved like one, but because that was all she left behind in her wake. The ghosts of her enemies. No one has ever seen her face. It was said that humanity could not handle her beauty. Her skin pale and her lips full and pink. Her eyes a dark blue that hid a wealth of knowledge and pain. Hair the color of ink that absorbed all light from a room. It was of the darkest black.

"Many people tried to find her, to prove the myths and the legends wrong, but no one could find her as she was a shadow and shadows went unseen. Then one day, by chance, the Ghost was found by a stranger, who was entranced by her beauty. She did not see him, but by some small luck, he saw her. He watched her from a distance; watched her move like a dancer and fight like a warrior. He watched as she would stop at nothing to get what she needed to save a person she loved. The man's heart sank to his stomach because he knew if she loved a man that much, he would never stand a chance. He would never be on the other end of her love. But being as transfixed by her beauty as he was, he couldn't help but approach her. She didn't trust him for how could someone who has never been seen by anyone before trust someone who did actually see them? It was unnatural to her. The feeling was unnatural to the man, as well. He didn't know what to make of it at first. Didn't know how he could tell her that he was on his own mission to get revenge. She was on a mission to save the person she loved, and he was on one to kill everyone in sight. There was a world of differences between them, but he couldn't resist the spell she put on him. It was intoxicating, almost like morphine or alcohol.

"To the man's surprise, she let him in. That mind of the shadow working overtime, never taking her eyes off him. She thought that she needed his help when, in truth, she didn't need anyone because she was the strongest person who ever lived. She made a name for herself in a world where the sun blistered skin, and Nighters tormented humanity. He was the one who needed her. Although he was too proud to admit it, he knew that he couldn't pull off his mission without her. Never without her. He never wanted to be without her ever again. He never wanted to be without her from the moment he met her at that little oasis.

"The man discovered that she was looking for a long-lost brother and not a lover. The man was overjoyed and made it his life's mission to win her over. She didn't make it easy for him." Meloni snorted. This man, the beautiful, incredible man. "She spent most of her time in her own head, talking to the shadows of her own mind. See, she's always been afraid of the unknown. She didn't like change. She knew that letting anyone new into her life would change her world forever. She didn't have many people who cared. Those that did got taken away from her. She was afraid of getting hurt and the man understood that much more than she could ever imagine. He tried his best to get into her head, to join her tango with the shadows, but she kicked him out before he could ask her to dance.

"Then one day, he took them on a detour to a part of

the wasteland he knew she had never seen before. It cost them an entire day, but he didn't care. That look on her face when she saw the magical oasis was worth more than any revenge he could ever get. They shared a moment in that pool, a moment that was stolen by evil men. She let her guard down, and it nearly cost her her life. He thought for sure that he had blown any chance he had with her. He thought that she would never speak to him again. Not after the vulnerable state he was responsible for putting her in."

Meloni sucked in a breath and continued the story for him. "But to his surprise, that was the part that won her over. He had made her vulnerable, but he saved her and had her back. She's always put up those walls to save herself as there was no one else around to do it for her. He proved her wrong."

Bryce grinned and kissed her forehead. "What happened then?"

"Take off your shirt. I'll show you."

FIFTEEN

A Different
Perspective

In the dungeon of the fortress, the Smuggler sat and thought about all the things he's done over the years. He thought about what he did to deserve the sister that risked her neck for months to save her. He would do it for her every day for the rest of his life, but he knew she was worth it. She knew that her heart was something this hell of a world needed. He felt guilty for isolating her from other people all her life. He knew that she was coming for him because she had no one else. He was all she had. At the time, he thought it was for the greater good, but now he wasn't so sure. She was his little sister. She wasn't supposed to protect him. It was supposed to be the other way around. It had been the other way around for as long as he could remember.

He accepted his fate a long time ago. He knew that he was going to die in the dungeons, or he was going to die trying to escape. He didn't have the hope of ever seeing his sister again. Not until now. Not until that strange man introduced himself as the Scorpion and claimed to be an ally. Not until he told Michael things about his sister that only she could have told him. He didn't believe that it was real until he described what she looked like and the determination she had to get him home safely. That was his sister, alright, and without him there, she had made some powerful friends in high places.

The way the man spoke of her was different, though. Something was off. He realized a little too late that the man was utterly infatuated with her. He would do anything for her, and Michael was a bit jealous. He was the one who was supposed to protect her, to help her, not some stranger. He failed, and another man stepped in.

He gave the man a means to escape, to get back to his sister, who was either dead or dying. He had planned to take the route himself too, but decided against it. They needed someone on the inside, and he wasn't going to leave the prisoners here to rot. He had to get them out. He knew that he had to be there for them to come back and save them all. If anyone stood a chance, it was the Ghost and the Scorpion. He knew that he was risking their lives. He felt guilty for it, but he knew that they were risking their lives traveling through the wasteland every day. This was no different. At least that was what he told himself to feel better.

In some way, he knew that they'd come back for the other people even if he escaped with the Scorpion, but his sister would be reluctant for him to join them. She had already lost him once; she wasn't going to stand by to lose him again. She didn't have it in her to risk the people she loved like that. It was what made her heart so beautiful.

He told the Scorpion that he didn't want to see his sister before the actual events of the rescue. Why? Because he was afraid.

He was afraid that he might chicken out when he saw her. He didn't want any reason to back out. To tell them that he could escape on his own and that they should leave. The people in the dungeons, the people taken by the Barracks needed them more than they needed safety.

He always thought the Barracks were a myth. He never thought the horrors he's heard before were all true. They were all as true as they could possibly be. It wasn't like the stories he made up to make the Ghost and the Smuggler more notorious. He did it because they needed the fame to get more money. No, this wasn't like those stories at all. In fact, he was sure that there were horror stories about the Barracks that were never told in the first place. They were a much bigger threat than anyone ever thought.

He's been in their dungeon for a week. He was waiting to get transferred to one of the other fortresses where he would be forced together with the other prisoners and whipped into submission to build the damned fortresses. The transfer was set to take place in a day or two, three days at most. Meloni and her friend had to get here before then. Once the prisoners were all manacled together, there was no chance of fighting back.

It was his job to rile them up. He whispered through the walls to the cells next to his. Telling them that help was coming. They had to spread the word. They had to get ready to fight back. To fight the men who tortured and killed so many of them. If only Michael could unsee what these people did to others. If only he could unsee blood coated chairs and instruments in the dungeons. If only he could unhear the screams of agony and the laughter from the guards that followed. They were the ones he'd kill last, he decided. When he had time to do to them what they did to the others. It was probably one of the things he was most excited about. Revenge was a dish best served over a long period of time and with sharp objects in his hands.

Along with riling up the prisoners, he had to figure out

a way to get the materials he needed to build a bomb. He wasn't called the smuggler for nothing. He could get things in the most unlikely places. It was how he made the bomb in the first encampment anyway. If only he had timed the damned thing better.

He would get the supplies when the other prisoners were doing their parts. All he had to do now was wait.

THE DAY HAS COME for the Scorpion to finally get his revenge. The day for him to avenge the death of his first love and his son that he loved so dearly. He wished that any of this could bring Nicholas back. He wished that Meloni had the chance to meet the little man. He wasn't sure how she felt about children, but Nicholas had a certain charm that was impossible to resist. Celise always said that Nicholas got it from him, but Bryce wasn't so sure about that. He didn't like to think that Nicholas got anything from him. He wanted the kid to be better than he was.

He looked over to where she still slept, her dark eyelashes fanned over her cheeks in a way that made his stomach flutter. She was gorgeous, she was absolutely gorgeous.

He found it hard to believe that she was as deadly as she was. He wouldn't think that face was capable of doing any wrong. It was the sort of face he imagined angels having as a child. He supposed she was an angel of some sort. The angel of death was still an angel.

Bryce had doubts about the day that was ahead of them. He spent most of the night tossing and turning. He was watching the sunrise now, and he knew that the following hours were going to be the most important hours of his life. He wanted to tell Meloni that he couldn't do it.

That there was no way that they were going to win. In a way, he knew that she would never accept that, and it would put her in more danger than she already was. She'd try to do it alone. Although she was a skilled fighter, she was still only one person. One person against an army of men that were trained like he was. He didn't tell her the full extent they went through to train their men. He didn't need her sympathy.

Their plan was littered with holes. He didn't know how to patch them. Even if they did win by some miracle, what then? What would happen to the soldiers? They couldn't kill all of them, and if they didn't control them somehow, there was surely going to be an uprising again. There was going to be a new general who might even be crueler than the current one.

"What are you worrying about?" A sleepy voice asked from next to him. Bryce sighed. His mind was too busy. He had to calm down. Nothing good ever happened with a mind that was thinking about a hundred different things at once.

"I'm trying to think of a way we won't get killed today," he admitted.

Meloni sighed and sat up, her dark locks draping over her bare shoulder. "We are not going to get killed."

"How can you be so sure?"

"Because no story has ever ended without the main characters having a taste of life together."

SIXTEEN

Thick Air and Master Plans

THE AIR FELT DIFFERENT AROUND THE BARRACKS' fortress. It made Meloni's throat feel tight and her chest heavy. Perhaps it was the event that was about to take place that made the air feel so thick. Perhaps it was the lurking, waiting to jump out at them. They weren't prepared enough for this, but she doubted they would ever be more prepared.

Meloni had put on the face of the Ghost for the first time this entire journey with Bryce. This wasn't a job for the skilled girl who grew up in a hole. This was a job for the Ghost, the girl of the shadows. She had shed the beige cloak when they got to the grate, watching for the black one that seemed to move on its own. She had to look the part even if she didn't feel like it.

She told Bryce that they weren't going to die, that they were going to make it through this, but she had her doubts, she knew that he still had his doubts as well. It was as if saying them out loud made them real and she couldn't risk it. Instead, she decided to be positive. To be the Ghost that no one could stop. She could get in anywhere. She could win every fight.

Bryce looked at her, his goggles hiding his eyes and the bandana the rest of his face. Even his head was covered by his hood. The Ghost and the Scorpion.

They were the Ghost and the Scorpion. She had to repeat that to herself over and over to remind herself that they were the characters in legends. They were the ones people feared, not the other way around. They were the Ghost and the Scorpion. They were the Ghost and the Scorpion. They were the Ghost and the Scorpion.

Meloni nodded at her partner as she pulled the mask over her face and hid her pitch-black locks under her hood. It was time. It was time to reunite with her brother and take down the Barracks once and for all.

Bryce lifted the grate. She squeezed through the small space. She was surprised that Bryce fit through it at all. Sailor's cussing from behind told her that it was a tight fit.

Sand crunched beneath her gloved hands and as much as she hated wearing them, she was grateful for them at that moment. Who knew what awful things hid in this small tunnel? She didn't want to think what sort of droppings she was crawling through.

"Don't think about it," the Scorpion whispered from behind as if reading her mind. Meloni closed her eyes and pushed through, crawling as fast and as silently as she could. She was grateful that the mask kept out most of the scent, as well. She didn't know how she would have survived if she had to suffer the full wrath of the aroma.

Finally, she reached the end of the tunnel, which seemed to be half-hidden. The grate on the other side was slightly ajar and she lifted it silently to see where they were emerging. They emerged beneath a bed, the thick blanket tossed haphazardly over the side to conceal the grate. Yes, this was it. It was only her brother that would think far enough to hide the grate. The man was a genius.

She crawled beneath the bed, the sudden shift from sand to concrete, an odd sensation on her hands and knees. Leftover sand crunched beneath her weight.

There was a shift on the bed, and she pulled a knife from her belt. Just in case they moved the prisoners around. Just in case it was someone else and not Michael.

"Stop lurking and get out here," her brother hissed in a whisper, and a wave of emotion crashed into Meloni. It felt as if she ran into a stone wall.

Without considering the consequence of noise, Meloni rushed from under the bed, discarded her mask along the way, and wrapped her arms around the man sitting on the bed. She breathed him in, absorbing the warmth of his body. Strong arms wrapped around her waist. She allowed herself to sob into his neck.

He was filthy and smelled wretched, but she didn't care. It was Michael, the person she hadn't seen in weeks and weeks. The man she had been so close to only a week ago but didn't bother looking for in the cells.

"Melbell," he whispered, his own voice cracking with emotion.

She didn't trust herself to speak, didn't trust herself to say anything, really. She just wanted to stay like that, holding on to him for a little bit longer.

Meloni felt a hand on the small of her back and knew who it belonged to. It was a subtle way of telling her to get a move on and that they didn't have much time. She could reconnect with her brother after the war was won. There was no time for all of the emotion now. It wasn't good for her focus either.

"I know this is a sweet moment, but we should get a move on," Bryce pushed and the siblings nodded, knowing that he was right. Meloni pulled away and looked at Michael. He was thin. She should have known better than to think they were feeding him.

"You can tell me how terrible I look once we're done," Michael laughed and picked up the mask that Meloni had dropped. She took it from his hand and nodded, still not able to speak.

The girl took a deep breath, swallowing the emotions of joy and fear, and then slid the mask back into place.

She became the Ghost once more.

SOME THINGS in life were just impossible to predict.

Meloni started this journey with a mission to get her brother back and a random medic who had to get to an outpost.

Now she was waging war on the most dangerous military base in the wasteland with the Scorpion and the Smuggler by her side. They were the big three. The three people to avoid at all costs. The three people you did not want to mess with. The three people who could kill a man, dispose of his body, and sell his organs on the black market before anyone even noticed he was missing. Meloni found irony in the fact that her plans had taken such a detour. She always worked with a plan. She always made sure she knew exactly what had to happen next and how it had to happen. This was something completely different. It was the biggest moment in her life, and she hadn't planned it. Never even thought about it. She was going to take down the Barracks with the man she feared above everyone else. The man everyone should have feared. The one man nobody should have messed with.

With a handful of prisoners behind them, most of

them underfed and weak, Meloni and Bryce snuck through the dungeons and added more people to their army as they went. They were growing at a snail pace, but that was alright because they haven't been seen yet. As long as they stayed in the shadows, they were all safe. For now, at least.

When the last cell door was opened, Michael hissed in her ear. "This is it then? This is the army?"

Meloni scowled. "This is the distraction we need to keep attention away from us." She turned to the prisoners who have added up to fifty-seven. Ten of them were women who hardly looked capable of holding a stick, while half the men looked half dead. She shuddered to think what it must have been like in the dungeon. What it must have been like to live underground for all this time? She doubted any of them even had the will left to live. "I know you have been to hell and back. We have come to save you, but you have to help us do it."

Bryce took his turn and spoke. "We need you to act as a distraction. Avoid combat as far as you possibly can. I don't care if you light stalls on fire or lure the sand wolves to this place, but we need a distraction if we are going to defeat the general and his men."

There were low mumbles of disapproval. Of course. Of course, they thought this was merely going to be a rescue mission. That they didn't have to do anything.

It was Michael who whispered at them to settle down, shut up, and listen. His whispering voice was louder than some people's normal voices and she quickly glanced at the gate to see if anyone heard them. No one came. "Do you want to die down here?"

The prisoners mumbled soft "No's," and Michael continued. "Then you are going to pull yourselves together and help us. We cannot do this alone. The Ghost and the

Scorpion are here to protect you and fight for you. Are you willing to do the same for them?"

His speech was beautiful. A little pretentious, but beautifully effective. Bryce looked at her in the dim light, grinned and nodded. "The Scorpion and I will head out first and take care of the guards that stand between the cells and the exit that leads to the courtyard. Once you're outside, make a mess. Make as much noise as you can. If you are capable of fighting, get a weapon and stand your ground. If you can't fight, then I suggest running and playing tag with the guards. Remember that this is a military base. No one is your friend. No one will hide you, no one will help you, and no one will show you any mercy. All of them are trained killers. You avoid them at all times."

They nodded reluctantly. It was all Meloni could hope for, really. She didn't need them to be enthusiastic. She only needed them to get out into the courtyard. That would cause enough chaos on its own.

"Right," Meloni said, turning to her brother as Bryce stalked ahead toward the gate that led to the hallway littered with guards. "You know what to do," she said, and he nodded. There was no one she trusted more with this task than her brother. Not even Bryce, with all his skills, could accomplish this.

"Oh, and Mel," he whispered before she lowered her mask over her face. "Don't get shanked."

She grinned. "I'll try my best not to."

IN COMPLETE SILENCE, one guard fell after another.

Meloni and Bryce moved in the shadows. They were completely invisible, using every column, every shadow to their advantage. One by one, they picked off the guards,

Meloni on the right and Bryce on the left. She couldn't see his mouth under his bandana, but she knew that he was grinning from ear to ear. He enjoyed these sorts of games. If she had to be honest, she enjoyed it as well. Especially if she was winning against miscreants like the Barracks.

When they reached the entrance that led to the courtyard, Meloni's knife was dripping blood. She cleaned it on her pants, the crimson liquid invisible against the blackness of the fabric.

"That's the sort of behavior that got your wound infected in the first place," Bryce hissed in a teasing way. She wished she wasn't wearing the mask so she could stick her tongue out to him. This was no place for such things anyway. This was serious.

As if sensing the sudden shift in her mood, Bryce took her hand in his and squeezed it. "Don't wimp out on me now, Ghostie."

"Me?" Meloni put her hand on the door to open it. "Never."

SEVENTEEN

A Big Boom

THE SUN WAS A LITTLE TOO BRIGHT WHEN THE DOORS TO the courtyard opened, but it didn't seem to affect the raging prisoners who stormed from the door.

The courtyard erupted into chaos. Meloni watched from the shadows as prisoners were cut down and shot by the guards. They were the ones stupid enough to try fighting them. The rest did their job beautifully. It looked like something from a movie. It was almost comical. They hit guards behind the heads and pulled on their cloaks, they pushed over stalls and made a giant mess of things. One man even had the balls to punch a guard in the back of the head and tricked him into thinking it was one of his fellow guards. Guards fought guards and the angry shouts could probably be heard all the way from the top of the fortress.

It was glorious. It was truly magnificent.

Meloni looked over to Bryce, who nodded at her. It was time. They had to make as much of a mess to lure the commander out of the fortress. It was no use killing him where no one could see. He had to be taken down in front of his men and by the person who he failed to kill for disobeying him. It was going to be poetic. It was going to be glorious.

Without another thought, the two of them joined the fight. They were much more graceful than the prisoners. They weren't seen until it was too late. They worked together like a well-oiled machine, their movements fluid as if they were one person. When Bryce ducked, Meloni swung a blade. When Meloni was holding a man down, Bryce shot him in the head.

Somehow in the chaos, though, they got separated. Meloni was left to fend for herself. It was easy with Bryce by her side. He knew their moves, and she moved with him. He knew their strengths and weaknesses. He used it to his advantage. Meloni hasn't had enough time to study them, to learn their patterns like she was used to learning.

Her blade swung and hit nothing but air. The guard had dodged her assault, and he was launching a counter. His face was contorted in anger. The veins in his neck bulged. Meloni took a step back, looking around the court-yard for anything to use, anywhere to climb to where she could escape his wrath. There was nothing around, and then his fist collided with her side. It shouldn't have been as painful as it was, but the wound that Bryce had so carefully nursed was now throbbing with the blow. Meloni fought back the tears and repeated the words that she's been saying to herself since she put on the mask the very first time.

She was the Ghost. She was the Ghost. She was the Ghost. She was the Ghost, and nothing could knock her down.

Meloni's nostrils flared and she feigned a lunge left. The guard moved to catch her, but she was too fast. She stepped out of reach of his tackle with quick feet and buried her knife in the back of his neck. She didn't watch him fall to the floor.

BRYCE MOVED through the crowd like a bull in a china shop, breaking everything he saw and touched. He had lost track of where Meloni was, which was a good thing. If he couldn't find her, neither could the guards. He had watched the guard punch her. It was as if she had forgotten who she was. It was as if she had forgotten everything she had learned over the years. Bryce ran to her rescue, but he stopped short when he saw her transform into the woman he couldn't get out of his head. He watched as she tuned into the Ghost and walked on shadows.

She killed the guard faster than his eyes could register, then she leaped and was gone. She disappeared before his very eyes. It was the first time he had seen it for himself. The stories were true. She really did have the ability to disappear at any given time.

Bryce heard a battle cry behind him. He relied on his sharpshooting abilities to defend himself. The bullet hit home in the man's chest and he fell to the floor. Another guard emerged from the one he had just killed, and when he tried to shoot, the pistol was out of bullets. He swore and lunged at the man. He hasn't had a decent fistfight in ages, and he was a little bit rusty. Taking on amateurs like the bandits was one thing, but fighting with men with the same training that he's had was a different story.

The guard punched him in the face and his goggles cracked, making it hard to track his movements.

"Goddammit," he swore and swung his left fist, waited for the guard to block it, then swung low with his right.

Bryce could hear the guard's rib crack as his fist found just the right spot above his stomach. The guard doubled over, and Bryce used the opportunity to move behind the guard and wrap an arm around his neck. Knowing what he was planning, the guard clawed at his arm, but his neck was snapped before he could do any damage to Bryce.

MELONI FELT like she was having an out-of-body experience. She's only ever read about it, heard about it from other people, but never considered it to be real.

Her body floated in the air as she lunged from guard to guard, using their bodies to push herself into the air. Her blades were a part of her, extensions of her arms as if they were fingers or hands. Wherever she stabbed, she found flesh, and bodies were littered behind her, leaving a trail of blood and death. She was death.

She was the Ghost.

AFTER WHAT FELT like an hour-long battle, three figures finally appeared on the balcony that overlooked the courtyard. The commander was flanked by two guards, two guards that Bryce recognized all too well. Those were the men that whipped Celise, the men that brought Nicholas to the commander, and the men that slit Bryce's throat.

There was a flame of rage in Bryce's stomach at the sight of them, and the sun couldn't compare to the heat inside his body.

With new adrenaline coursing through his veins, Bryce sprinted toward the balcony. He dodged fists that reached toward him, sliding under and jumping over obstacles. He was rage. He was fury.

From the corner of his eye, he could see a black shadow moving toward the balcony as well. She matched his speed.

The commander took a step back from view, but they were already there, there was no escaping Bryce's wrath now. The wrath of a lover, the wrath of a father. The wrath of a human being demanding justice for what has been done to his people. This ended here. This ended today.

This was going to end with the commander's head at his feet and a shadow at his side.

This was going to end with the fall of the Barracks.

MELONI SCALED the wall that led to the balcony, expertly finding her footing in the grooves of the stones. Her gloves ripped as she gripped the stones, and her finger-tips bled. She didn't even notice. There was only one thing ghosts felt, and that was rage.

The Scorpion and the Ghost reached the balcony simultaneously. One clad in black and one dressed to blend into his surroundings. It was a duo that no one ever thought was possible, but a duo that worked so well together.

Meloni stalked toward the guard on the left while Bryce targeted the right. She knew that these were the men who caused Bryce so much harm. She could see the cruelty on their faces; she could see the face of a scared little boy in their eyes. The little boy they had killed as an example. The innocent little boy who didn't ask to be in this world. The boy, Nicholas, who must have looked at his father with teary eyes and a shaking lip. Meloni didn't bother shaking the image from her head as she pounced like a lioness. Her prey stepped back, but she was too fast. Her blade had cut through his jugular faster than he had time to scream. Her only regret was that she didn't have more time to carve him up like he did with so many others.

From the corner of her eye, she saw that Bryce was on top of the other man, his fists raining down on his face until the man was motionless. Only when his screams stopped did Bryce look up from the mess on the floor. His gaze fell on the commander, and Meloni swore she heard a whimper.

He tried to run, but the duo was too fast. Meloni stood in front of the door, blocking his way. He turned to go in the opposite direction, but Bryce was there. He grabbed the commander by the neck before pulling his bandana down and lifting his goggles. The commander's face twisted in fear. Meloni could see the satisfaction in Bryce's face. She could see the ideas he had with this man. How he could make him scream and beg for mercy the same way he had screamed before the commander shot his son.

"Remember me," Bryce purred. His voice as poisonous and slick as a sand snake.

"The traitor," the commander hissed breathlessly, clawing at the hand around his neck. He drew blood, but the hand stayed firm. Bryce squeezed.

"The father you forced to watch as you killed his son," Bryce corrected and tossed him to the floor.

The commander gagged and gasped for air. Meloni wondered if he knew that it was the last breath of air he was ever going to breathe. She wanted to tell him that. She wanted to bathe and soak in the look on his face when she told him. But it was not her place. Instead, she looked at the position of the sun. It was time.

She found Bryce looking at her.

The Ghost nodded at the Scorpion.

Bryce picked the man up by the throat again and dragged him to the very edge of the balcony where everyone below could see. His voice boomed through the walls of the fortress and, as if miracles still happened, the crowd turned to look at him.

"Today, this man dies by the hand of a man that has suffered his cruelty. Many of you know who I am. I grew up with you, I have trained with you. Many of you have taken part in whipping my woman and watched as this man shot my son. Many of you have never seen me, but you may know me by another name," Bryce curled his lip as he spoke. As if he was disgusted by what he was saying. "You have tortured and killed many innocent people because this man told you to. Today you will watch as I kill him, and you will watch this empire fall."

MICHAEL STOOD at the entrance of the tunnel that led to his old cell. A packet of matches in his hands. It was easy enough to get the things he needed to build the bomb; the problem was building it in such a short amount of time. He hoped the fuse was correctly connected, and he prayed to any god that would listen that the duct tape would hold everything together. The duct tape barely had any stickiness left, which is why he had to tie it like a ribbon.

There was still fighting. He could hear the gunshots; hear the screaming and battle cries. He could hear it all and was grateful that he wasn't a part of the fight.

Mel's plan was genius. It was symbolic, it was well thought out, and it was pure, damn genius.

The fortress housed the plans for other fortresses. It

held the documents of the slaves that they have gathered and housed a good number of guards. The supplies the Barracks needed to survive were all housed in the main fortress building. With that gone, with the dungeons nonexistent, there would be nothing left for the Barracks to return to. The other fortresses would get no supplies and without production, they had nowhere to go.

The plan was so good because even if they failed for some reason, Michael would still blow up the fortress. He'd still take away all the supplies they needed to survive. It would be at the cost of his sister and the Scorpion, but at least their deaths wouldn't be in vain.

Michael looked at the sky, looked at the sun that he had taken for granted his entire life. He never knew how much he'd miss the sun if he were kept in darkness for that time. He planned on never taking the sun for granted again.

He watched as the sun reached its highest point, prayed that his sister was as far away from the main building as possible, and lit the match.

He watched as the fuse ran into the tunnel at a rapid speed, and Michael followed suit, running in the opposite direction.

BRYCE PULLED the commander back from the edge and shoved him to the ground after his speech. The crowd was silent, awestruck. Two people, it took two people to take down a tyrant and his entire army. She wondered what sort of silence it was. Was it a raging silence that threatened to erupt into angry shouting, or was it the sort of silence that came with defeat? She sniffed the air, focused her hearing on the silence. The latter, she thought. It better be the latter, or every single guard here would feel her wrath. She had so much to hand out. It was hard to decide where she was going to start.

Meloni watched the sky intently. Ten seconds... Five seconds...

On cue, the duo ran toward the ledge of the balcony, leaving the commander on the floor. They leaped into the sky, just as an explosion went off behind them. Meloni's cloak caught fire and she could only imagine what she must have looked like. Death incarnate with the flames of hell following her through the sky.

The heat was intense. When she hit the floor, she ducked and rolled. Her cloak was discarded before it could do any damage to her skin. It wasn't planned, but she was happy it happened. The crowd made a half-circle around her, watching her. Most of them had ducked away from the explosion, but the braver ones crept closer. The remaining prisoners cheered, and a smile crept onto her face.

She turned to look at the crumbling fortress. Meloni felt Bryce's presence next to her before she saw him. It was a strange shift in the air that only happened when he was around. It was as if her body was in tune with his and responded to each other without them even realizing it. Knowing he was next to her eased a tightness in her chest that she didn't even know was there.

He took her hand in his. Lacing their fingers together like their lives have been intertwined the past two weeks. She hardly had any fabric of her glove left and she could feel his pulse in her hand. It was steady. There was no rush, no rapid heartbeat. It was nothing like hers. His heartbeat was as calm as if he had just woken up from sleep. It was strange, but she came to expect the unexpected from him.

The fortress was nothing but rubble in mere seconds, and the commander was buried beneath the stones. Meloni hoped he was still alive as flames ate what remained of the fortress. She hoped he was trapped under the bed he made. She liked to think that she could hear a faint screaming through the fire and the chaos around them.

Meloni looked at Bryce, and she knew that he thought the same.

EIGHTEEN

The Aftermath

MELONI WATCHED THE HUSTLE AND BUSTLE OF THE CAMP from the window of the container.

There were people of all occupations, working together to rebuild their lives.

When they took over the Barracks, Meloni wasn't sure about what would happen next. She didn't allow herself to think that far. Hope got a lot of people killed and she intended on staying alive as long as she possibly could.

Bryce took charge without a second thought, and she wondered briefly if it was his plan all along. She realized that he hadn't planned any of it, but instead, it was instinct to him. It was an instinct to lead, to rebuild, and to heal. He was a doctor, after all. Healing was what he did. He was working toward peace; the thing he always thought was a myth. Meloni smiled at the thought.

Michael didn't stay at the fortress. Meloni was sad to see him go back home to the hole, but she knew that it was his place. It was where his friends were, where Carter was. It was where he had built his entire life. Meloni thought that it was her life too, until she met Bryce. She then realized that it was only the idea of home and not the actual thing. She found her home with Bryce, and wherever he was, she would go.

When Michael left, it was a teary and wet cheek affair. Meloni didn't know how she was going to survive without him. He told her that she was doing just fine. It was the truth. She was still alive and she was happy. She was doing better than fine. At the last minute, Meloni remembered the dog tags and handed them back to Michael. He looked surprised that she still had them. Through everything that she's been, she had held on to them the entire time. She gave him her tags too. She didn't need them anymore. It was a part of her past that she had outgrown in the past month. It felt good to let go.

"They're really working hard," Bryce said as he snaked his hands around her waist to kiss her neck. "I never thought I'd see the day the guards lifted a finger."

Meloni smiled. They gave the guards a choice. Join their cause or die.

It seemed harsh, but they couldn't let them go. Not people as skilled as they were. Their skills were valuable and could be used in rebuilding the wasteland. Their skills could be used when taking down the other fortresses and freeing the slaves. Their crimes were forgotten, but they got no special treatment. They worked just as hard as the old prisoners that were now free and decided to stay under Meloni and Bryce's rule. Word had spread about the Ghost and the Scorpion's identities, and that they took down the Barracks single-handedly. No one dared challenge them, but it was going to come sooner or later. Everyone wanted a piece of them. Wanted to say they defeated the great dynamic duo.

The duo was ready for whatever may come their way.

"You never told me the end of the story," Meloni said, smiling to herself.

"What story?"

"The story about the Ghost and the man that was desperately in love with her."

"You mean the man who defeated all odds and got the girl in the end?"

"I don't think we're talking about the same story," Meloni turned around to look at him, putting her arms over his shoulders. He bent over to kiss her, and she could taste the fruit salad he had for breakfast on his lips.

"After they defeated the evil wizards in the fortress, The Ghost decided that it was time to let go of her doubts and trust fully in the Scorpion."

"That doesn't sound right either," Meloni protested, and Bryce rolled his eyes.

"After the wicked king in the castle made of stone was defeated by the dynamic duo-"

Meloni shook her head. "Nope."

"When," he started.

"Try again," she purred in his neck, kissing his neck.

"You little minx," he said and picked her up. She wrapped her legs around his waist and kissed him again. Her hair fell like a waterfall over his head.

"Do you want me to tell the right version of the story?"

"Go ahead." Bryce set her down on the bed, his body between her legs as he kissed her jawline.

"To the Ghost," she started, pushing him away from her slightly so she could look at him. "There was never a place she was happier than next to the Scorpion. When he wasn't around, she longed for his touch, for his kisses, and the butterflies in her stomach that followed every smile he gave her. She knew she loved him from the moment she saw him but was too stubborn to admit it. She knew that she would be his queen in whatever way he wished to rule his kingdom. She knew that he would be a just and fair king to the wasteland, and she vowed that she'd do everything in her power to put him on the throne. For what was a queen without a king?"

Bryce grinned down at her, dimples forming in his cheeks. "Well, historically speaking, more powerful."

Meloni groaned and rolled them over, so she was on top of him, glaring down at him. "You are ruining the sweet, amazing story."

"On the contrary," he shrugged. "I believe that I have just added an interesting twist to it. See, no one would expect the queen to get rid of the king."

"This queen will never get rid of her king," Meloni retorted.

"Is it because of my dashing good looks, my amazing stories, my charm?" Bryce thought for a moment, and then added: "It's my body, isn't it?"

"On second thought, maybe it is time the Ghost got rid of the Scorpion."

"Meloni, honey, you have gotten rid of my venom the moment I met you. I've been the pet you keep in your pocket ever since."

Meloni's heart exploded and then she kissed him. It was a long and passionate kiss. A kiss that took her breath away. That made everything make sense in the world. It was the sort of kiss that got the fire burning in her stomach and it couldn't be extinguished by anyone but Bryce. "Let's see if the Scorpion can still sting without his venom."

About the Author

Renee Joiner has been in love with the supernatural for longer than she can remember, so it is no surprise that she is an author of paranormal urban fantasy. Although she discovered her passion for writing when she was only twelve years old, she didn't make her writing debut until many years into the future. Adventurous and fun-loving, she enjoys traveling to new places, exploring new sights and meeting new people. Thus, she delights in creating fantastical worlds that are sure to give her readers an escape from the real world while simultaneously providing thrilling entertainment.

Besides her special knack for writing, you'll also find a passion for metaphysics spirituality which she has been nurturing for over four decades. Renee hails from New York and currently resides with her husband in their empty nest—unless you count their three adorable fur babies—in Florida. She enjoys adding to her sea of knowledge and thus spends her free time learning new things.

To find out more about Renee Joiner, feel free to visit her **official website**.

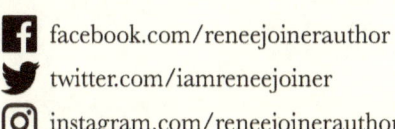

facebook.com/reneejoinerauthor

twitter.com/iamreneejoiner

instagram.com/reneejoinerauthor

More Books by Renee

Dark Huntress Series
Glen Cove
The Witch
The Djinn
The Countess
Magic of the Night Series
Raven Magic

Thank You...

Thank you for reading my book!
I really appreciate all of your feedback and I love to hear what you have to say. Please leave your review at your favorite retailer!